THE LABYRINTH

GOURAHARI DAS

Translated from Odia by MANORANJAN MISHRA

THORNBIRD
NIYOGI BOOKS

Published by
NIYOGI BOOKS
Block D, Building No. 77,
Okhla Industrial Area, Phase-I,
New Delhi-110 020, INDIA
Tel: 011-26818960, +91 7428978881
Email: niyogibooks@gmail.com
Website: www.niyogibooksindia.com

Editor: Anwesha Panda
Design: Nadeem Ahmed
Cover design & illustration: Amit Malhotra Design Studio

ISBN: 978-81-19626-90-8
Publication: 2025

Printed at Niyogi Offset Pvt. Ltd., New Delhi, India

There is no witness so terrible and no accuser
as powerful as the conscience which dwells within us.

—SOPHOCLES

1

Draupadi was never so timid, not even in her childhood. As a child, she would cross dark streets alone in the evening hours quite comfortably to reach their neighbour's house. During sunny summer afternoons when the streets were deserted, and the chirp of crickets shot through the air from the fields surrounding the village, creating dread in the minds of mischievous children, mothers would force them to lie down for a nap warning them that otherwise ghosts would appear. Draupadi dared crossing the streets alone to reach the pond at the end of the village. She would sit under the shadow of the *gulmohar* tree and throw pebbles into the pond. An intelligent student, she never hesitated to answer the teachers' questions, whether they were aimed at her or not.

She wondered how this sense of dread, which couldn't deter her during her childhood, overpowered her after she had grown up.

Draupadi felt there was a strong connection between responsibilities and dread, just as there existed one between wealth and hazards. During childhood, she was not smothered under the weight of responsibilities. Those days, her parents took all her responsibilities upon them. Her elder brother's twin assurances, 'Don't worry. I'll replace whatever you demolish; I'll get you what you need,' always comforted her. These days, she lives in a city alone. The responsibilities of raising a small child rests on her. Concerns about her husband, who lives far away, hang heavy on her mind. Were not these enough to constrict her?

Of course, she had been used to Debadatta's absence. She no more complained about it. Whatever complaints she had were but temporary outbursts. However, she had never thought that she would have to live away from her husband for such long spells.

The rickshaw carrying Draupadi had reached near the school gate. She dropped Pintu there and was returning to complete the unfinished chores of the morning.

But suddenly she opened her mouth. That was her mistake.

Later she would realise that it wasn't wise on her part to give in to momentary impulses like that.

Before she realised how to respond, the words had already slipped out of her mouth. She shouted loudly, 'Hey, what's happening there?'

Draupadi's words angered the bearded man who had parked his motorcycle by the curb and sat on it. His look reflected utter vexation at the fact that an unknown woman was unnecessarily poking her nose into his affairs.

The face of that person seemed to emit fire. His bearded face looked menacing, like the face of an angry chimpanzee. The long red *tilak* on his forehead glistened with sweat. He was wearing a black shirt and matching black trousers. He held a chain in his hand and looked around for signs of danger.

They were three in all. The bearded man sat on the motorcycle, keeping watch on the passers-by for any signs of danger. The other two dragged the boy and hit him mercilessly. Blood ran from the mouth and nose of the victim. Exactly at that time, Draupadi had reached the school to fetch her son.

At first she thought that the young men were fighting over some trivial issue. Such things were quite common in a city. Almost every day, one would come across such incidents on the street. Like wild bulls, young men from different lanes would fight each other.

Draupadi knew that the young men couldn't be faulted entirely for this state of affairs. She accepted Debadatta's arguments on this point. What would these young men do if they had no way to channel their energies? These had to be spent anyhow and fighting among themselves was the only option left for them.

Today however these young men weren't fighting amongst themselves. The two strong and stout looking ones had dragged the 25-year-old and flung him onto the ground in front of the bicycle repair shop. One of them was repeatedly punching him on his stomach, back, thighs and face and the other one was approaching him aggressively with a shining sharp knife. It was then Draupadi yelled, 'Hey, what's happening there?'

Draupadi's yelling alarmed the two youths. The young man with the knife stabbed the one on the ground two times in the stomach before fleeing to the motorcycle. The bearded young man had already kept the engine on. He turned on the accelerator and they sped away.

Draupadi stood frozen. The distressed and pathetic wailings of the man shot through the air. The surroundings reverberated with his bitter cry, 'Oh Maa! I am dying.'

People present in the vicinity soon rushed to the spot and surrounded the man. Draupadi turned from her rickshaw-seat and found a crowd there. She could not figure out where these people were a moment ago.

She could not sleep that night. The gory scene flashed before her eyes time and again. The miscreant, while fleeing from the spot, had stared at her threateningly. The bearded man's look was the most menacing one, as if he was not a human being looking at another but a snake staring at a frog, ready to swallow it whole.

Drops of sweat moistened her hands and feet. Her entire body shivered in anxious dread. Although the incident took place in front of hundreds of people in broad daylight on the crowded Stewart School Road, people distanced themselves deliberately from it. Draupadi realised that by not distancing herself from it like others, she had exposed herself to the butcher's knife. Now there was no escape from it.

Draupadi found it difficult to believe the man who had telephoned and introduced himself could really be the Inspector of Nayapalli Police Station. She doubted that it could be a plan by the three young men or their team leader either to issue threats, extract information or to gauge her intensions. She was reminded of the conversation she had with him.

'Yes,' said Draupadi.

'Who is it? Is that you, Draupadi madam?'

'Yes.'

'I am the Inspector-in-charge, Nayapalli Police Station.'

She shuddered at the word 'police'. She gathered herself and said, 'Yes, how can I help you?'

The man who claimed to be a policeman spoke from the other side, 'We need your help in connection with the Stewart School Road murder case.'

She wished to put the receiver down on the stand and get done with it. But she didn't and asked instead, 'Help! What help?'

The man continued, 'You can recognise the culprits if you see them, can't you?'

She had lost her patience by then. 'I have seen nothing. Nor do I know anything about the incident. Sorry,' she replied and disconnected.

The telephone rang once again.

This time without giving her an opportunity to respond, the speaker said, 'You seem to be an intelligent women. Of course, it is natural on your part to behave that way when your husband works in another town and your child has to go to school alone. If you ever change your mind, do call me.'

While she continued saying 'hello hello' into the mouthpiece, the man on the other side had hung up. She was now certain that it wasn't a call from the police station but rather the hoodlums were after her. If she had remained silent like others, she would never have to face such adversities. But by then, it was too late.

The sight of the murder flashed before her eyes. Never ever in the past had she seen so much blood. Blood ran down in a stream from the young man's nose. Blood gushed out the moment he was stabbed in the stomach. She had only seen so much blood in a fish and mutton market. The fish-vendors, instead of cleaning the blood of the cut fish with water, dab the blood on the other fish yet to be sold. The patches of blood on them, would make the fish they appear fresh.

But in this case the blood didn't belong to a fish. It was of a human being. The sight of that blood had made her feel agitated. That compelled her to scream.

She now regretted that mistake. Every day many such incidents take place all around the world. Hundreds of people witness these but they behave as if they have seen nothing. They are considered wise and clever. It would have been wise on her part as well if she had gone away turning a blind eye. Had she not howled as she did, it would have been better. She would have lost neither sleep nor her peace of mind. She felt restless like a perch fish being tossed on a hot pan.

She was certain that the hoodlums had collected all information about her and that they must be keeping an eye on her movements. She would never be able to escape their clutches.

Draupadi pulled Pintu to her lap. He slept peacefully. Without any worries. But sleep eluded her.

Her mind kept dithering about the next course of action. Should she send a message to Debadatta? Should she write to her father? She could never stop Pintu from attending school. Should she take a few days' leave from office? She couldn't decide.

Her heart began racing, and her breathing became more shallow. The anxiety of an unforeseen accident haunted her. She kept asking herself as to whose inauspicious face she had seen that morning. How to come out of the mess was her top priority now.

Despite her best efforts, she could not forget the terrifying sight. She could neither erase the innocent face of the victim nor forget the grotesque motions of the criminals. How in a matter of seconds can one be murdered! That too a human being! The entire episode looked like a scene from a horror movie. She ran her palms across her hands, face, eyes and nose. No, this was not a scene from a film. This was real, and something that she had actually witnessed. The inside of her head throbbed. She asked herself anxiously, 'What would happen now? How would things shape up?' Thinking about it in a loop made her restless. Lack of sleep compounded the problems.

Draupadi opened a drawer, put her handbag in it, and arranged the files properly on the table.

Mr Nayak, a colleague, arrived. He let out a boisterous laugh although there was nothing to laugh about. He fingered the edges of the papers lying on the table.

The man always behaved like that.

Draupadi spoke in an agitated voice, 'What are you looking for?'

'Ma'am, for your kind information, Akhil Babu won't come to office today. He rang up the BM to inform him. BM was asking for you.'

Draupadi felt vexed. This Akhil Babu had been a headache ever since he had joined the office. He has the habit of taking leave quite often. He was on leave last week and he has gone on leave again.

'When was the BM asking for me?' said Draupadi and waited for the answer. When she didn't receive any, she turned around to leave. Mr Nayak had already left by then. 'What a strange person!' she thought and started for BM's cabin.

Mr Sahu, Kartik and Manjushree of the sales section were gossiping loudly. Narottam had taken a break from cash counting at his work station to join them. Draupadi heard Mr Sahu talking about yesterday's murder.

'This city has become extremely unsafe. How can someone live in peace knowing people are getting murdered in broad daylight?'

'It has far surpassed Bihar in terms of the number of murders,' remarked Kartik, the union leader.

'How could three youths commit a murder and escape despite the presence of so many people? Were they human beings or puppets? What a spineless lot!'

Manjushree had joined their branch a few days ago. She was unmarried. Her beauty made her the centre of attraction.

Young men buzzed around her throughout the day. Kartik's words made Draupadi angry.

'As if he would have pounced on one of them if he had been there!' she thought to herself and left.

The Branch Manager said, 'Akhil Babu has gone on leave. The audit team is expected anytime. Please get the papers ready and have a discussion with me thereafter.'

Draupadi did not argue with him. Her discontent with Akhil Babu was intensifying. In view of the troubles she was in, she was thinking of going on leave for a few days. But, how would she tell her problems to the manager now?

The Branch Manager was a young man. He was younger than her. He said, 'Anything else, ma'am?'

Draupadi said, 'I want to apply for leave…'

The Branch Manager suddenly grew solemn. The smile that had played on his face a moment ago suddenly vanished. 'No…no. How would I manage the branch if both of you go on leave at the same time? You should sit down and make a proper plan together.'

Draupadi walked out of the manager's chamber.

Mr Sahu, Kartik and Manjushree were still busy gossiping. Mr Sahu needed no encouragement to start proselytising. He had the uncanny ability of commenting on something or the other throughout the day. His interest chiefly lay in the sale and purchase of land. His only concern was how to earn more money. Earlier, he was into the share market. After the stock market had crashed, he switched over to sale and purchase of plots. Most of the time, he was surrounded by his colleagues. Most of the staff members sought his assistance while going ahead with the sale or purchase of landed property.

Kartik held a newspaper open.

Draupadi enquired, 'What are you reading?'

While handing the newspaper to her, Kartik said, 'Take it and read. Three hooligans stabbed a young man to death near Stewart School yesterday. Doesn't your son study at that school?'

Draupadi almost snatched the newspaper from him and started browsing through it. Kartik was telling the truth. The young man had succumbed to his injuries. Police had no clues about the murderers. The culprits were absconding.

Draupadi strode back to her seat. There was a tsunami of unsettling thoughts in her mind. What a serious blunder she had committed! If the culprits attacked her, what would she do? If they abducted her son…

There was no solution in sight. Every moment she suspected that some evil would surely befall her. The culprits had already got hold of her landline number. It was possible that they would inflict some harm on her. In their attempt to silence her, they might try to eliminate her. Or, they might blackmail her.

How could they get her phone number? Draupadi was clueless.

If she somehow got the number from which the phone call was made, she would have some clue as to who had made it. Who could help her get the number?

All of a sudden, Draupadi remembered Mr Senapati. When she took the phone connection, Mr Senapati had helped her. If he wanted, he could help her in getting the number of the callers.

Pintu had not gone to school. Draupadi had left him with a neighbour while coming to office. She had rung Debadatta in the morning to inform him of all that had happened. But he didn't have a phone. Their neighbour, Mr Nanda informed her that he was'nt there. For a second, Draupadi was worried as to where he had gone so early in the morning and why. But then, she changed her mind. Perhaps it was a sign that God didn't want her to pass this news to him. Otherwise, why wouldn't she have got through to him?

Why bother Debadatta with these things? He stayed far away. He would only get worried about them. Besides, what news would she convey to him? That she had invited trouble for herself? Known for his irritable temper, he was sure to fly into a rage. Over the last few months, he was constantly distressed about the issue of his transfer. He had stopped visiting them every weekend. The fresh trouble was sure to disturb him.

Draupadi was able to trace Mr Nayak after a thorough search. She got up from her seat and said, 'I am leaving for the telephone office. If the BM asks for me, please inform him that I shall be back in half an hour.'

Mr Nayak said, 'Madam, please come back quickly. There's the cricket match between India and Sri Lanka.'

Draupadi tried to keep her cool. What did he think of himself—Gavaskar or Kapil Dev? Would the sky fall down to earth and break into pieces if he didn't watch the match for a day? Did he come to the office to work or to watch cricket? She kept quiet. Was her leaving for the telephone office not personal work?

In a manner of making a promise, she said, 'Don't worry. I'll surely come back in half an hour.'

Mr Senapati was extremely busy that day. The two phones on his table rang constantly. He would pick them up at times and say a few words into the receiver before hanging up. Besides, there was a heap of files and important papers on the table. Five customers sat surrounding him in visitor's chairs. A look at their faces revealed that they had urgent business.

Draupadi stood near the door and said, '*Namaskar* Mr Senapati,'

Mr Senapati flashed a smile, 'Please take a seat.'

There was not a single chair vacant in that room. Draupadi looked around for one and kept standing. Mr Senapati felt a little awkward and loudly called out to a peon, 'Hello! Anyone around? Get a chair for madam.'

The youngest of the customers got up from his chair, looked at Draupadi, and said, 'Madam, please have a seat.'

Draupadi thanked him for his kindness and said, 'No… no…it's all right. You please sit.'

Mr Senapati spoke to the young man. 'There is a cable fault in your part of the city. It'll take a couple of days to mend.'

The distressed young man said, 'How come the cable is getting damaged so frequently! Please do something.'

'What can I do if there is a fault in the cable? Can't you see how people are digging the streets wherever they like? What can the department do? Forget about theft, here even murders are being committed in broad daylight. Who and where should we complain?'

Draupadi fell into an anxious reverie once again.

The young man said, 'Okay then…do as you wish' and left. Draupadi took the seat vacated by him.

She didn't want to discuss her problem in the presence of so many people. She wished a little privacy. However, the moment she took the chair, Mr Senapati looked up at her face, 'How can I help you? Is your phone out of order?'

Draupadi nodded her head. She was soon struck by an idea. If she requested Mr Senapati, he could easily disconnect her phone. In that case, no one would be able to ring her up or issue threats.

However, she couldn't tell Mr Senapati what she had in mind. Customers visited the telephone office to get their phones in order. No one visited it to get his phone disconnected.

Mr Senapati repeated. 'Yes, madam! How can I help you?'

Draupadi felt annoyed with the people sitting around his table. If their problems had been solved, they should leave. What was the use of unnecessarily idling around, occupying the chairs?

She said, 'It's something personal.'

In an attempt to pass the hint to the customers who sat around him, Mr Senapati said, 'Okay, I'll discuss your problem with the GM today. However, if you don't make any payment, it won't be possible to provide uninterrupted connection to the booths.'

'STD booth owners,' said Mr Senapati in a manner of introducing them to Draupadi and then said, 'Would you like a cup of tea?'

Draupadi politely refused. She had lost her appetite since yesterday. She felt exasperated as she had not a wink of sleep last night. Her head reeled and she felt like throwing up.

'For the last few days, I have been receiving some bogus calls. The calls came two times yesterday. Can't we identify the number from which those calls come?' Draupadi enquired.

Mr Senapati smiled and felt reassured. This was not a problem he was supposed to deal with. Had Draupadi's phone gone out of order, the responsibility of setting it right would have rested on him. He enquired, 'What kind of calls? Vulgar?'

Draupadi flinched within. Arranging her saree carefully she said, 'What do you mean?'

'I mean vulgar calls! Most people receive such calls some time or the other. Once my wife received one such call. She informed me later.'

Draupadi was taken by surprise. Do telephone office people receive such calls too? Then she thought to herself, 'Why shouldn't such calls come to them? Had it not been so, there would be no thefts in police officers' houses and no patients in doctors' families.'

Mr Senapati added, 'There is no dearth of perverts in the world. They derive much pleasure from such nonsense. Hadn't Khushwant Singh written that the Indians are a sex-starved tribe. You know…'

Draupadi responded, 'No…no…I didn't mean such calls. I am receiving threat calls.'

Mr Senapati looked more reassured. He said, 'In that case, you have no problem at all. The call that my wife received was a vulgar call. Even she was ashamed of discussing with me the language that the caller had used.'

Draupadi kept mum. She didn't know much about Mr Senapati. Has she not found herself in grave trouble, she wouldn't have come to him at all.

She continued, 'Someone rang me up twice yesterday and said that he was making the call from the local police station. He left a number with me too.'

'Do you have the number with you? Tell me the number. If we ring up, everything will be clear,' said Mr Senapati with a lot of enthusiasm.

However, Draupadi had completely forgotten the number. Despite the best of her efforts, she could only remember a few digits but not the entire number.

Mr Senapati said, 'You should have noted down the number immediately. Okay, tell me what sort of threats he was issuing you?'

The truth refused to escape through her lips. She knew very well that if she divulged the truth, she might invite unnecessary trouble. If the message was somehow leaked to the miscreants, they would never allow her to live in peace. They would destroy her family.

Draupadi said, 'Nothing in particular. The caller was only talking nonsense.'

Mr Senapati said, 'It won't be possible on our part to ascertain where the call had come from. Please submit a written application. We will put your phone under observation.'

Draupadi didn't want to submit any applications. All that she wanted was to get some information about the phone number without inviting any further trouble.

Mr Senapati looked into her face in utter confusion. He picked up the phone lying on the table and remained engaged in some conversation. Putting the receiver back he said, 'Please leave your number with me. Let me see what I can do. Please listen…when such a call comes, tap the switch hook twice while continuing the conversation. In that case, the operator at the exchange will try to locate the callers.'

Draupadi felt a little relieved.

Mr Senapati added, 'In such cases, cellular phones are very helpful. One can get the number of the caller on the phone itself.'

Draupadi continued to remain thoughtful.

She was getting late. She got up and said, 'Thank you very much for your help. Sorry for the trouble I have given you.'

Mr Senapati flashed a smile and said, 'Madam, you have forgotten to give me your phone number.'

An embarrassed Draupadi mumbled, 'Four-one-five-eight-three-six,' and left.

It was very hot outside the telephone office. She felt hotter as she had just come out of an air-conditioned hall. She looked around for a rickshaw.

On the other side of the road, near a betel shop, stood three young men with a motorcycle. The moment Draupadi's eyes fell on them, she felt as if she saw a snake with its raised hood. She returned to the office and stood on the verandah, keeping an eye out for them. The bearded young man resembled the young man who was an accomplice in the murder.

Draupadi realised they had been keeping a watch on her movements. They had followed her to this place. She felt utterly helpless and deprived of strength as to what to do. They were staring in her direction and whispering among themselves. She guessed she must be the subject of their conversation. Her head reeled. She decided to return home and send an immediate message to Debadatta. Things had gone beyond her control.

The three young men sped away with their bike and disappeared. Draupadi heaved a sigh of relief while thanking God.

2

Debadatta said, 'Hasn't Pintu gone to school today?'

'No. A street-fight broke out near his school yesterday. The rickshaw-puller hasn't reported on duty today.'

'What sort of fighting?' a worried Debadatta asked.

Draupadi was on the verge of telling him the truth but suddenly thought that it would not be right to disclose that she herself was an eye-witness of the incident. Debadatta might get too worried about their safety or he might lose his temper. Maintaining her cool, she said, 'A young man was murdered by unknown assailants.'

Debadatta said, 'These days, one has to encounter similar problems everywhere. The same is the case here too.'

'What happened there?' an anxious Draupadi queried.

'No...there's nothing to worry. I'll reach on Saturday next. Do take care of yourself.'

'What about your transfer?' asked Draupadi.

'No. Not much progress. I'll share the details with you later. Whatever is destined will happen.'

Draupadi wanted to reveal many things but couldn't. She felt as if someone held her by her throat, constricting her.

Debadatta said, 'Do you want to say anything else?' Since Draupadi remained silent, he hung up as five more people were waiting outside the booth.

He emerged from the booth, paid for the call charges and left.

For some mysterious reasons, his talk with Draupadi was somewhat awkward. He didn't want to continue the talk as it would cost more money.

In his mind he abused the senior officials of the Forest Department in filthy language and headed towards the restaurant.

As usual, three or four people were standing near the restaurant with a low asbestos roof. All of them belonged to the coastal districts. Debadatta smiled at them and asked the waiter for food.'

Debadatta was not much interested in the food. He had received unconfirmed information that he was being transferred to Banei.

He had already spent fifteen years in the job. He had been transferred from one jungle to another, from Keonjhar to Kalahandi, and from Kalahandi to Sundergarh. He had seen sal, piasala, mahua, teak and tendu trees change their colours many times. On the contrary, he did not find time to share the joys and sorrows of his family.

When the question of transfer came to his mind, Debadatta felt like revolting against the system. He would often wish to relinquish the job and go home. What was the use of working under a system which did not care for one's weal and woe, one's joys and sorrows? Every time he hoped that he would be transferred to a place near Cuttack or Bhubaneswar so that he would be able to take care of his old parents, wife and son, he would be disappointed. And this time too, there was no hope.

Debadatta was enraged with his colleagues who had spent years with favorable posting at Cuttack or Bhubaneswar. He was perplexed to think how they managed all this. They just moved from one place to another at their convenience for a few months before returning to the former place of posting.

Mr Patnaik, who had joined him, was transferred to Nandankanan. He had purchased two plots in Bhubaneswar. He was now constructing a building on his Kananbihar plot. He sought transfer to Bhubaneswar on the ground that his wife was ill. Debadatta knew quite well that he sought transfer so that he could construct the house. He somehow had developed wonderful rapport with the higher-ups in the department.

Debadatta never sought a transfer so that he could construct a building at Bhubaneswar. He didn't want to build one house after another and rent them out to people. He was happy in the house that he had taken on rent. After retirement, he would settle down in his village to take care of his parental property and live in peace. He wasn't interested in living in the city. It would be difficult for him to adjust with city people. He only wished to spend some time with his wife and son. However, no one listened to his request.

Debadatta finished eating. He took out his handkerchief, wiped his face, promised to pay the bill later and came out of the restaurant.

Last time when he had visited Bhubaneswar, he met the CCF. He also carried with him the application written by his father. The CCF indifferently looked at the application. He only turned the pages. Fixing his eyes on the curtain, window, and files he said, 'You may go. I'll look into it.'

Debadatta said, 'Sir, I have never troubled you with unnecessary requests. I will be obliged if…'

Interrupting him at once the CCF said, 'You should have joined the Secretariat service. The government can't create a jungle in the heart of the city just to post you here. You may go now. I'll look into it.'

For Debadatta his statement slid like a hot knife into butter and rubbed salt on his wound. He came out of the CCF's chamber and kicked in the air. What a brute the man was! He didn't even read the application once.

Mr Mangaraj was right when he said that all officers were hypocrites. They talk of rules, regulations and idealism but lick the feet of ministers and secretaries. They have no time or desire to solve the problems of common people.

Had he been an IAS or IFS officer, would the CCF have treated him so disdainfully? Certainly not. They were governed by a separate set of rules. If a senior officer's wife was posted somewhere in Sambalpur, he would be posted in Bargarh. If husband was Collector of Bargarh, wife would serve as the MD of Bargarh's IDCOL cements. If the husband was posted as the Superintendent of Police of Jharsuguda district, the wife would be placed as the Superintendent of Police of Sundargarh district. If the wife was transferred to the Secretariat, the husband would be transferred to the Heads of the Department building. If the husband was sent on deputation to Delhi, his wife would be sent there too. This special treatment was meted out to them because they were senior officers. Only they were endowed with hearts, youth and desire. The subordinate officials had nothing to boast of—neither youth nor desire. They are impotent fellows. Let them stay away from their wives. Let them live like logs of wood in teak wood forests.

After he had entreated several times, Debadatta was once posted at Rajnagar. Although it was in Cuttack district, it was situated far away from the Cuttack city. He would have been happier if he had been posted at Baripada instead. However,

Debadatta didn't complain. What was the use of raising a hue and cry? The officers of the Forest Department were of two types. Some of them were like tigers and bears; the others were like *sal* and teak wood trees. The former took a great delight in issuing threats and creating fear in the minds of the subordinates. They were devilish like wolves. The others neither heard one's prayers nor promised anything. Like the trees of the forest, they were left to their agony and suffering.

Draupadi hardly understood the complexities of the world. She would ask at times, 'When your colleagues are getting transferred to their places of choice, why isn't it so in your case?'

Her words would make Debadatta angry. He would yell at her in frustration. The first of the two-day holiday would be spoiled by the bickering whereas the second day would be devoted to brokering peace. He would return to Phulbani while she would stay back at Bhubaneswar.

This morning Digal visited Debadatta in his office. Debadatta was browsing through the file concerning Digal at that time.

Digal dragged a chair himself and spoke insolently, '*Namaskar*.'

Debadatta had an opportunity to witness his impudence.

Digal continued, 'Why have you seized my truck on false charges? Do you know the amount of loss I incur every day?'

'It's not my business to calculate your loss,' replied Debadatta.

Digal's nostrils flared up in anger. Debadatta knew very well that he had political connections with the high and mighty. A dreadful beast! He combined the ruthlessness of savage animals and the cunningness of businessmen. Debadatta chose not to unnecessarily engage in an argument with him. It was Digal who incited him.

Digal shouted, 'Complete the paper work soon and release the vehicle. Otherwise, there will be trouble.'

Debadatta was flushed with anger by then. He found it difficult to relish that a timber mafia had entered his office uninvited and was issuing him threats. He got up and spoke gently, 'Otherwise, what would you do? Would you transfer me from this place? Go and do whatever you wish to do.'

Digal was ready for retaliation. He threatened him, 'I can do that in the twinkle of an eye. Do not play with fire...'

'What will you do?' Debadatta burst out in anger.

'Ask your wife to pray for your well-being,' the young man who accompanied him said threateningly.

Debadatta had lost his cool. He was ready to give him a befitting reply. At this time, his guard rushed in, placated Digal and the two young men, and took them out of the room. With his eyes burning in disdain, Digal yelled, 'Bloody fool! Talking of rules and regulations to me. If I simply give so much as a hint, my henchmen would kidnap your wife and child within minutes…Talking of law. Just wait, very soon I'll teach you a lesson.'

Debadatta sat down with his head resting on his hand. The words of Digal continued to disturb him even hours after he had left. He could not decide what to do. Had Digal not had political connections, he would have slapped him on his face. Only because of that he was compelled to restrain himself.

Receiving threats was nothing new in this profession.

He had received such threats many times before. The timber mafia were dreadful beasts. If they wished, they could mercilessly slaughter anyone who stood in their way. When he was posted at Rajnagar, he had received such threats from the goons of the ruling party. Fortunately, nothing happened till he left the place on transfer.

Debadatta had learnt from experience that there were great differences between a businessman and a politician. The politicians were weak people; they could be pacified easily. Since they were weak, they made a lot of noise. 'Empty vessels sound much.' However, businessmen like Digal weren't weak. They possessed huge amount of black money; they enjoyed immense political patronage. There was hardly any need for people like him to yell. However, Digal had yelled. He had combined business with politics. If he introduced himself as an adivasi leader at one place, he presented himself as an industrialist somewhere else. His behaviour had made Debadatta desperate and angry.

He had complete details of Digal's business. He also knew that the threat issued by him wasn't an empty one. If he wished, he could do him great harm.

How would Debadatta surrender himself before his threats? He didn't wish to become a hero. He knew such ambition was foolish. But, how could he accept the dictates of the timber mafia while donning the uniform provided by the government?

He was reminded of his childhood days when he was a high school student. He was a student at Patapur High School. The school was a few miles away from his village. So, he had to stay in the hostel. The name of the hostel cook was Bhaskar. The boarders fondly called him 'Bhaskar nana'. In addition to being the hostel cook, he doubled as the school peon. He managed both his responsibilities with effortless ease.

About twenty-five students stayed in the school hostel those days. The boarders were children of either low-caste harijans or poor farmers. Rice, *dal* and mixed vegetables were served to them twice a day. Each boarder had to contribute fifteen kilos of rice and thirty rupees per month for the purpose.

Despite the contribution, the quantity of rice served to each student would prove insufficient. Bhaskar nana would lose his cool if someone asked for some more rice. '*Seta peta na gadia, haan*? (Is that a stomach or a large hole, eh?)' he would mutter. 'If you contribute only fifteen kilos of rice for the entire month and consume half a kilo cooked rice in a meal, where from I am supposed to get the extra rice?' he would say.

The children were compelled to go half-hungry. Some of them approached the headmaster with this complaint. He however paid them no heed.

He would advise them, 'Eat less, so that sleep won't come to your eyes and you will get more time to study.'

For a long time, Debadatta didn't understand the connection between going half-hungry and education. But he was certain about one thing. The head-master never discussed the matter with Bhaskar.

The head-master would fly into a rage when someone complained that they were being fed with watery *dal* and boiled gourd in place of boiled potatoes. 'Such items are extremely healthy', he would say. 'Even pregnant women are served with these dishes keeping in mind their nutritious value', he would argue. Since neither Debadatta nor any of his friends had the experience of being a pregnant woman, they didn't dig into the matter any further. The children concluded that since Bhaskar nana was hand in gloves with the headmaster, it was no use complaining against him.

The Superintendent of the hostel also didn't support the children. He would rather say that he had himself tasted the dishes several times and he found them tasty. He believed that no other hostel in the vicinity would be serving such delicious dishes to its boarders. The children had no option but to listen to the advice, half-hungry. However, they would always devise some plan against Bhaskar nana to expose his malice.

Bhaskar nana reared a calf. He would bring the calf along with him when he'd come to school. He would tether it to a peg in the school field and go to the hostel to cook. He would light the hearth, put the rice cooker on it, and leave the rice to cook. In the meantime, he would go to the field and cut grass. He would pilfer a portion of the daily ration and hide the *dal*, rice, potatoes and onions, neatly wrapped in his cotton towel, and place it in the sack along with the grass. No one had an inkling of it.

One day, Debadatta caught Bhaskar nana red-handed. While Bhaskar went to the office verandah to ring the bell, Debadatta discovered the packet in the grass-filled sack, took it out, and kept it hidden.

That day when the children asked for some more rice, Bhaskar repeated his old sermons.

On reaching home, he didn't find the packet.

Debadatta remembered the incident quite well. Since it was winter, he slept on a bench on the verandah. A couple of boarders were washing their clothes on the cemented verandah.

Bhaskar nana came running to him, took his hand in his own and was apologetic. He spoke about his poverty and vowed never to do it again. His fair face had turned lustreless and he looked pathetic. Debadatta took pity on him, let go of the opportunity to turn a hero, and returned the packet.

When the incident flashed in his memory, Debadatta would smile. He would take pity on him for being childish. Petty thieves like Bhaskar nana were caught red-handed. With folded hands, they begged to be pardoned. But, thieves whose crimes were far more serious in nature, demanded audaciously that the rules and regulations be changed in their favour. Even officers, in collusion with them, changed the dates on the circulars to justify their immoral activities.

Society holds such people in high esteem. They are greeted by respectable people. They are invited to address the public from podiums. Small children receive their certificates and awards from their hands. Their parents exhibit these photos on their drawing-rooms.

At times, people cut tender branches to use as tooth-brushes. They cut wood to light the hearth or to use these as beams supporting a thatched roof. When such people were arrested by the guards, he was reminded of Bhaskar nana. He would take pity on such people. However, he never let them go scot-free. He would throw away the bundle of wood from their head or the pieces of logs from their shoulders. He would threaten to sue them if they engaged in such illegal activities in future.

But with the people like Digal, he was helpless. A timber-mafia like him dared enter his chamber and issue him threats and he watched on helplessly. Had some higher officials of his office not supported him earlier, he wouldn't have dared doing that. If he had gone ahead to trap him, these officers were sure to come to his aid. They would weaken the case against him.

In the newspaper that morning, he had read about the conditions laid down by the dreaded sandalwood mafia of Karnataka, Veerappan. The news made him seethe in anger. The shameful surrender of two state governments at his feet was a cruel mockery of law.

Debadatta knew of the three hundred forest guards whom Veerappan had murdered. He shuddered thinking about the fate of their families. They must have read the news. They must be blaming their fate and spitting on the poor system of justice.

The news of Digal having threatened him with dire consequences must have spread like wildfire in the entire town. For a small town like Phulbani, there could not have been a more sensational news. Digal and his accomplices would be boasting of their audacity. The bastards thought if the news spread far and wide, Debadatta would feel humiliated and shrink within. His confidence would be shattered.

At times he thought it would be better to bow down before these anti-social elements. Who would he bank on in his fight against them? He knew that people like Digal enjoyed the patronage of big companies as well as the support of people in power. This shattered his confidence.

Digal's threat kept ringing in his ears. He would boil in anger at the thought of it. What vulgarity he displayed while issuing the threat! He would go crazy at the thought of it.

With who would Debadatta share all these things? Who would he seek support from?

He was reminded of his wife and son. It was good that Draupadi stayed at a far-off place. Otherwise, she would be shuddering in dread by now.

Debadatta reached his residence. Laxman Reddy sat on the verandah smoking a *bidi*. At the sight of him, Reddy rushed to open the gate. He was burning inside with anger. He didn't wish anyone to notice the smoke that emanated from within.

He said, 'Switch off the lights and go to sleep.'

3

While fishing out the bunch of keys from her bag, Draupadi called out, 'Pintu, get ready quickly…it's already 9:15.'

Pintu was busy tying the shoelaces. He replied, 'I'm ready, Maa.'

She shut the doors and windows. The maid hadn't come that morning. So, she was a little late in getting ready. She had to drop Pintu at school on her way to office. She would pick him up after his school got over at four and go back to her office. They would head home together only when her work was over.

Yesterday, she visited a friend Kalpana, who lived in Chitrakut Colony. The two friends met after a very long time. Kalpana, on seeing her at her doorstep, said, 'Oh, what a surprise! Are you still alive? I thought you had died long ago.'

Draupadi didn't say anything in reply. Of course, she hadn't visited her for the longest time, but Kalpana could have paid her a visit.

Kalpana's husband was busy reading a newspaper. He had been working in a big industrial house in Bihar earlier, but had recently joined as the personnel officer of Nilachal Steels at its Bhubaneswar office.

At the sight of Draupadi, he said, 'How surprising! We are meeting after a long time.'

Draupadi responded with a faint smile and sat down.

Kalpana's husband was very friendly. The moment she sat down, he started, 'Do you know? Bihar is much better than Odisha in many respects.'

Kalpana remarked immediately, 'Might be true but people are murdered almost every day there.'

Without feeling defeated Kalpana's husband said, 'Despite such incidents, it's a much better place. Incidents happen quite openly there and not on the sly as they do here. If one gets angry with another, he fires at him openly. But he doesn't harm others.'

'Everybody takes bribes there,' remarked Kalpana, putting the tea cup on the teapoy.

'Those who take bribe don't forget to do your work. In Odisha, they take bribes but speak of morality and idealism and forget to do your work. That's never the case in Bihar.'

'Why did you leave such a noble place, then?' said Kalpana mockingly.

'Only for your sake. If you send six letters in a month, how can someone concentrate on the job at hand? I was really very comfortable there.'

Kalpana chose to remain silent. She sat near Draupadi and said, 'I was really afraid. How can one live in peace when everyday one hears of murders and bombings?'

Draupadi nodded in agreement.

Kalpana continued, 'He was getting a good salary there. You will be surprised to know that a bribe of forty-five thousand rupees was changing hands through him every month. It went to everybody starting from the DIG to the *chowkidar*. What's the use of such money? Isn't life more important?'

Draupadi was reading the horoscope page from the newspaper. Earlier at the sight of this page, she would turn over to the next page, calling it useless. She was under the impression that the predictions never came true. But she went through each prediction quite seriously yesterday.

Kalpana asked her, 'What is your *rasi* (zodiac sign)?'

Draupadi replied, 'There are two—one as per the horoscope and the other as per the date of birth.'

'The newspapers take date of birth to make predictions,' said Kalpana's husband.

'I am interested in both.'

'What a joke! How can one person have two zodiac signs?' asked Kalpana's husband flashing a smile.

Draupadi said, 'My date of birth is 18th February. I don't know exactly when I was born. I also don't know whether my zodiac sign is *kumbha* (Aquarius) or *mina* (Pisces). So, I go through the predictions in respect of both. I go for the one which makes favourable predictions.'

'Just like me,' said Kalpana. 'I also go through the predictions under both—the *rasi* as per my horoscope and as per the date of birth. The predictions turn out to be wrong most of the time.'

The predictions in respect of Draupadi's zodiac weren't favourable. Both of those predicted *ghatachandra*, the waning moon—an inauspicious period. According to the predictions, the family was going to face disasters and suffer physical agony. In anger and dread she pushed the newspaper away.

Kalpana queried, 'Have you visited Sadanand Baba's ashram? His new ashram is close to your colony. He is an extremely witty person.'

Draupadi had heard about him although she had never visited his ashram. She asked, 'Have you gone there yourself?'

'I go there every day. I feel at peace with myself if I spend some time there. Why don't you go there? You can feel the difference very easily.'

Draupadi asked, 'Where is Suresh Bhai posted these days?'

'Why? What business do you have with police officials?'

Draupadi kept quiet. She dreaded that Kalpana might misinterpret the whole thing. If the matter gets leaked and somehow comes to the hands of the culprits, there might be serious trouble.

She said, 'No...No...there's nothing serious. I just wanted to know his whereabouts.'

'He is posted at Rourkela these days. He was transferred only on the fifteenth of last month. He rings me up at times. If you have any message to send to him, you can give it to me.'

However, Draupadi didn't reveal anything and left soon afterwards.

The rickshaw reached the Stewart School square.

Draupadi looked at the spot where the incident had taken place last Monday. A police constable stood guard there. Although business was as usual in nearby shops, she felt as if a strange aloofness had engulfed the entire area. People shrank in some unknown fear when they passed it.

She felt a strange sensation gripping her heart. For some obscure reason, she felt as if the public present there would recognise her and ask her about the incident of that day. Without getting down from the rickshaw, she said, 'Pintu, I'll be here exactly at four. Wait for me. Don't come out of the gate.' Clutching his water-bottle in his hand, Pintu ran into the school.

Draupadi told the rickshaw-puller, 'Take me to Sadananda Baba's ashram.'

The rickshaw-puller seemed a little confused. Draupadi repeated, 'Ashram.'

4

Draupadi was visiting the ashram for the first time. She entered through a huge gate and reached an enormous bungalow. Numerous buildings stood surrounding it. One of those resembled a temple. At its summit was placed a golden *kalash* with a red flag flying atop it.

She reached a hall where Swamiji sat on an altar. He was giving sermons to an audience who sat surrounding him. She went inside and sat at the back.

Sadanand Baba was sermonising, 'When you reach the summit of a mountain or the roof of a skyscraper, you feel like taking a plunge downwards. In the same way, when you reach the foot of a mountain, you wish to climb it up within minutes. Man can never put up with one who is higher or lower than him. However, everybody can't take the plunge. Only the intelligent ones can. They don't take into account gains and losses. On the other hand, most people can't do it as they only calculate the gains and losses.'

She failed to make head or tail of what he was hinting at. He had matted locks, and his moustache and beard had turned gray. His beard covered his chest and reached his stomach. He looked like the typical sages in posters.

Baba Sadanand continued, 'Those whose queries have been answered need not thank me. The simple reason is I don't need to be thanked. When you pass from darkness to light through a door, do you thank the door? I have played the role of a door only. I am leading you from darkness to light.'

Draupadi was growing impatient. A feeling of worry and anxiety made her restless. An unknown caller rang up last night too and introduced himself as a policeman. She put the receiver down without saying anything. She knew quite well that the miscreants were following her. If they got an opportunity, they wouldn't hesitate to kill her. She found it difficult to hide her fears and anxieties. She needed a little consolation and support.

The sermon was over. She went near Swamiji and touched his feet. With downcast eyes, she stood in front of him, wondering how to explain all that had happened. Swamiji looked into her face with confusion.

She began, 'I am confronting a terrible calamity. I need your help.'

Swamiji replied, 'That is the wish of God; we are but helpless creatures. Come tomorrow. Come in the evening. I'll certainly try to find a solution.'

She wanted to say something more. But his disciples arrived. One of them brought his wooden sandals and kept those at his feet. Another one held Swamiji by his hand and made him get up.

He got up. She realised it wouldn't be possible to consult him anymore. She decided to leave.

She remained absent-minded throughout the day at office. During the lunch break, she rang up to Mr Senapati and said, 'Last night, there was a similar call. I tapped two times the way you had asked me. Please look into this.'

Mr Senapati replied, 'I will need some time. Please call me after reaching home. I will have made some enquiries by then.' She returned to her seat.

Mr Nayak was busy talking to his friend. She didn't appreciate his prolonged conversation when he had a lot of pending work to do and the audit team was expected to arrive any time. However, she didn't like to interfere. Her own condition was no better. Despite the best of her efforts, she wasn't able to concentrate. She was constantly reminded of the miscreants and their threats.

She thought it would be better if she wrote a letter to her mother. If her mother allowed Sushila to stay a few days with her, she could breathe in peace. There were so many people at home, if Sushila was away for a few days, there wouldn't be much trouble.

However, she was uncertain whether Sister-in-law would allow Sushila to stay with her.

Her sister-in-law was jealous of her. Last time when she visited them at the village, she made fun of her saying, 'You have put on a lot of weight. Perhaps that's because of the double income. You seem to have no worries.'

Draupadi couldn't decide how to respond to what she said. When she was unmarried, this sister-in-law of hers made fun of her by calling her lean and thin like a sheet of paper. She further pointed out that since she was quick-tempered, she didn't put on any weight. She was now taunting her for having put on weight. If she put her down those days, it was jealousy that prompted her to do so. Her attempt to belittle her today was also an offshoot of that feeling.

Her sister-in-law hailed from Cuttack and was extremely cunning. In the past, she easily avoided backlash by calling her a hot-tempered girl. She never ever told her directly that she was vicious. What she really meant was that if she had been good-natured, she would be keeping well. Draupadi never failed to understand her insinuations. She clearly understood her motive when she said that she had put on a lot of weight. Debadatta must be making a handsome income from his posting as a forest officer. Otherwise, she wouldn't be putting on weight.

Had Draupadi so wished, she could have answered her back but she didn't. Her love and concern for her brother prevented her from doing that.

Her sister-in-law had no children. She would fast and offer worship to gods throughout the year. She consulted physicians and took medicines prescribed by them. She consumed not only Ayurvedic but also Homoeopathic and allopathic medicines. She put on amulets and stone-rings seeking a cure for her infertility. In the meantime, sixteen years had passed but there was no success. Draupadi got married only a year later. Her son Pintu would be eleven soon.

Her sister-in-law hardly sent any gifts on Pintu's birthday. Draupadi's brother would make a clandestine visit the day before his birthday to avoid the displeasure of his wife.

Sister-in-law would fly into a rage when there was some discussion concerning a child. 'Had I wished, I could have become a mother long ago,' she would say. It was her husband's fault if she remained childless.

Draupadi's brother would never accept the allegations but he never said anything hurtful.

Sister-in-law said that after their marriage her husband asked her to go for an abortion. They didn't want a child to enter their lives so early. They wanted to have some more fun. Now that she had some gynic problem, everybody pointed their accusing fingers at her.

Brother had a different story to tell. He said that he was posted in Assam those days. The whole of Assam was burning in the fire of terrorism. He had to change his accommodation every six months. They would have faced immense trouble if the delivery had taken place at that time.

The exchange of words would often lead to a war.

In his attempt to make peace, Draupadi's father would say, 'Leave everything to God. Without His grace, not even the grass grows.'

Sister-in-law did feel hurt at times. Last time Father said, 'Don't worry. Pintu is there to offer the ceremonial *pinda*.'

An aggrieved Sister-in-law rushed back to the kitchen. Draupadi took Father to task and said, 'You have grown older, true, but there is no end to your childish behaviour. What was the need of talking like this in front of Sister-in-law?'

Father realised that he had been indiscreet.

Draupadi put off her idea of writing the letter. If she wanted Sushila to be sent to her, Sister-in-law might object. It was her problem and she should find a solution to it. Why should she be the butt of other's attack?

Mr Nayak's friend had departed in the meantime. He said, 'Madam, some unknown miscreants have abducted a child from the Shastri Nagar area of the city. We were discussing that.'

Draupadi was left dumbfounded. It was as if someone hit her with a hammer. She looked at her watch. It was a quarter to four. She said, 'Mr Nayak, please mind the office. Let me get back my son from his school.'

Mr Nayak nodded his head to indicate 'Yes, sure.'

A disturbing thought suddenly struck her. If those miscreants kept a watch on her movements, they would certainly be keeping a watch on her child. She didn't want to unnecessarily scare her child. If the child felt scared, it would leave an impact on his psyche. Besides, Debadatta lived far away. If for some reason Pintu felt scared, it would be difficult to manage things.

If she could arrange a maid, she would feel extremely relieved. But despite her best efforts, she had failed to arrange one. Cooking dishes in the morning, responsibilities at the office, dropping Pintu at his school and picking him up back again, his studies, and cooking again for dinner kept her extremely busy throughout the day. She felt breathless with the amount of work she had to do. However, none at her parents' house or at her in-laws' house expressed any concern. On the contrary, they would often say, 'If you are having so many problems, why doesn't one of you relinquish your job? How long will you continue like this?'

Draupadi found it difficult to respond to the question. She released all her anger and frustrations on Debadatta. He would console her, 'Obviously when both the husband and the wife work, they have to face many troubles. Don't take the accusations of others to heart. The problems will be solved once I am transferred somewhere here.'

The much sought-after transfer didn't happen.

Fifteen years passed in the meantime.

When such thoughts crossed her mind, she would take pity on herself. Was such a life worth living? Like a wheel, she whirled from morning till night.

Boys and girls, donning in school uniforms, emerged from the compound. They dispersed in all directions like bees emerging from the hives. Some of them ran helter-skelter, with their hands outstretched. Someone else kicked the grass in the school field. Someone's water bottle slipped off his shoulder and fell on the ground. Someone else's bag had come off. Someone had started pouring water from his water-bottle; someone else disposed of the food packed from the tiffin-box, unnoticed. They came out tasting freedom like birds uncaged.

Draupadi looked for Pintu from among the hundreds of similar-looking children. It was getting difficult for her to identify him from a distance.

She had spent her childhood in a remote village. While they were students of a village school, there was no need for uniforms. Children had the freedom to wear anything they could afford. Teachers didn't object if they carried different sized bags. They didn't carry tiffin boxes or water bottles. No one escorted students to and from school.

There was Pintu! Draupadi ran a few steps towards him. Like a passenger picking up his bag from the conveyor belt at an airport, she dragged Pintu by his hand from the queue. Pintu had to turn back again and again to say goodbye to his friends. Draupadi said, 'Why are you getting so late these days?'

Pintu was not interested in answering the question. Hundreds of students were still standing in the queue. Their parents were still waiting in rickshaws, scooters, motorcycles, cars and jeeps to pick them up.

Pintu, however, didn't express his thoughts.

The moment they took their rickshaw, Pintu told his mother, 'Did you hear, Mother? Last Monday, a murder took place near our school. The victim must have passed away'

Nudging Pintu on his thigh with her elbow, Draupadi said, 'Stop all this nonsense. Do you go to school to study or mind all this nonsense?'

Pintu was going to add something more but his mother's indifference held him back.

Draupadi prayed to God silently, 'Oh, God! Please protect Debadatta and Pintu. It hardly matters what troubles I have to face.'

When Draupadi felt desperate, she was reminded of her mother. The old lady would always say, 'If you have the grace of God, no adversity can weigh you down.'

Mother would often express her displeasure as Draupadi found no time to offer up prayers to Gods. 'If one doesn't heed elders and spiritual guides, he is sure to invite a great calamity,' she would caution her. After Monday's incident, she was reminded of mother and her advice more intensely. She felt guilty as she had criticised the so-called spiritual gurus.

Mother was right. 'Without God's grace, the child in Uttara's womb might not have been saved from the weapon shot by Aswasthama.' Draupadi beseeched Lord Krishna to protect her child with His Sudarshana Chakra.

Draupadi had no idea as to what the child-catchers did with the children they abducted. Some people believe that the children were sacrificed at the altar of the deities. Before large bridges and barrages were constructed, contractors offered the blood of such children to the deities. How would pillars be constructed in water? Some others believe that these abducted children were sold in foreign countries. These tales were enough to make Draupadi shudder in terror.

As usual, two scooters and a cycle were parked in front of the house of their neighbour, Mr Sasmal. Mr Sasmal was an engineer. He had two grown-up daughters and a son. Only because of them, the road leading to Draupadi's house was always jammed. Mr Sasmal's daughters were shameless. Although they were grown up, they preferred spending their time with boys. Draupadi wondered why the Sasmal couple didn't object.

Draupadi reached the door and unlocked it. The *madhumalati* vine had fallen off its support. She didn't help it onto the trellis. Instead, she went in and switched on the lights.

All of a sudden, something fell on her with a thud. While Draupadi stepped back to dodge it, she dashed onto a chair and slipped. When she turned back, she found Pintu watching her, with a smile on his face.

'It's a cat,' said Pintu.

Draupadi's heart drummed loudly. She thought perhaps someone had entered their house in their absence and hid inside. She shuddered.

She plonked down on the bed. Since the doors and windows were shut, the inside looked dark. She put on the switch. The entire house bathed in white light. She told Pintu, 'Go and change your uniform. Let me get some food for us.'

5

Debadatta was pouring tea from the saucepan. Just then, he heard the sound of the main grill-gate being opened. He looked in that direction and saw his colleague Mr Mohapatra coming in.

He poured the tea in two cups, put a cup on the table, and said, 'Please come in, Mr Mohapatra. What a pleasant surprise, that too so early in the morning too!'

While locking his scooter Mr Mohapatra said, 'I thought you might because of on some work. So, I am here to meet you.'

Debadatta handed him over the other cup of tea. He wondered what had brought him so early in the morning. He said, 'Where would one go in a place like this? The entire bazaar spreads over a small place between the college and the bank.'

Mr Mohapatra said, 'Have you been transferred to Banei?'

Debadatta didn't want to lose his cool so early in the morning. Suppressing his anger he said, 'Let the bastards send me wherever they want. How can one expect a

Cuttack–Bhubaneswar posting when one works in the Forest Department?'

Mr Mohapatra nodded his head.

Debadatta said, 'Alright, so tell me what is the matter? What ails you?'

Placing the tea-cup on the table, Mr Mohapatra said, 'I'm in great trouble. I don't know how to come out of it.'

His trouble didn't upset Debadatta; strangely, he felt happy from within. Why shouldn't he, when the entire world had turned a deaf ear to his troubles? Moments later he realised that he should not laugh at the misery of others.

He asked, 'What trouble are you in? Have you also been transferred to a far-off place?'

Mr Mohapatra was lost in thought. Debadatta took the cups to the kitchen and came back.

He began, 'The bloody rascal is causing much trouble.'

'Who?'

'The fellow who lives near my plot of land. He is stealing my bricks and sand. Besides, he does not allow the masons and workers to work in peace.'

He got the picture now. Mohapatra was talking about the construction of his house at Bhubaneswar. He had purchased a plot of land at Ratnakarbagh. While buying it, he had kept it a secret from Debadatta. Now that he was in trouble, he had come seeking help.

'How selfish such people are!' Debadatta thought to himself. When the times are good they hardly care for others. They arrive only when they are in trouble and pretend as if they are the most wretched people in the world.

'What else is he doing?'

'The water-pipe was laid by his house. He has deliberately damaged the T-connection. Consequently, the construction work has stopped for the last three days.'

'Anything else?'

'His children are hurling stones at our out-house. One of my workers was living there. He has left for his village to avoid trouble. He does'nt want this hassle.'

Debadatta found nothing abnormal at all in what he had heard. Such things keep happening in the city. Those neighbours who are supposed to help you when you are in trouble, cause unnecessary headache. Society is full of such debased fellows.

'Why don't you file an FIR in the police station?'

He smiled faintly, 'That fellow himself works in the police department. That's why he dares to indulge in such nefarious activities. Who will listen to me if I complain against him?'

He sounded helpless. In their own department, he was known for accomplishing difficult tasks with effortless ease. A very cunning person! He could sway the opinions of others—from a small employee to the boss, in his favour. Such a person was in grave trouble now. How ironic!

Debadatta replied, 'The problem lies right here. We all behave as if we are all kings of uninhabited islands. We hardly try to understand the problems of others just as others fail to understand that of ours.'

Mr Mohapatra looked blank as he failed to understand what Debadatta was hinting at.

Debadatta wished to lay bare his heart. Mr Mohapatra's problems were not exceptional; they were normal. Whether one lives in the village or in the city, one encounters such troubles. Even if they live in the same neighbourhood, they hardly know each other. The problem is more acute in the cities and towns. In the name of paying a visit, the neighbour really marks the quality and make of fans, fridges, TV sets and other such household articles. He feels hurt if the neighbour has better things; if they are of a poorer quality, he feels immense pleasure. If the neighbour's son performs well in the examination, the credit goes to their ability to manipulate; if his own child succeeds, his hard work is given credit.

In the manner of giving advice he said, 'Can you do one thing?'

Mr Mohapatra's face lit up. He felt as if his advice was going to bring an end to the problem forever.

Debadatta said, 'Do you have any connections with local hoodlums, someone who can plant a few slaps on the cheeks of the gentleman's son?'

Mr Mohapatra suddenly turned glum-faced. 'No, I don't know anyone. By the way, do you know anyone?'

Debadatta burst out laughing. All city people are like that. They hesitate to shoulder their own responsibilities and are always on the lookout for someone who can carry it out for them. Whether it concerns renting out their houses or finding a job for their children, they thrust the responsibility on someone else than carrying it themselves. During the next meeting they would ask firmly, 'What about the task I had given you?'

Mr Mohapatra also belonged to the city.

Debadatta continued, 'In that case, do one thing. Sell the plot of land. Search for another one somewhere else.'

Mr Mohapatra's face visibly dimmed. He complained, 'What sort of a solution is this? After a frantic search, for months on end, I had landed on this plot. Where can I get another suitable one? Besides, I have already spent forty thousand rupees in laying the foundation. Who will I sell it to now? After the entry of builders, land prices have skyrocketed. Is it possible for one to find a litigation-free land these days?'

'What will you do then?'

'That's what is worrying me. Perhaps this man was eyeing this plot of land. He wants me out of his way.'

Debadatta kept mum.

Mr Mohapatra whined, 'You don't understand my problem because it's mine and not yours. Had you been in my place, you would have understood it well.'

Debadatta mumbled to himself, 'How would you know if I have problems or not? Everybody in the world has some problem or the other.'

After Mr Mohapatra left, Debadatta closed the gate and walked back into his house. He was reminded of his father, mother, brother, sister-in-law, Draupadi, and Pintu. Before marriage, he had promised to do many things for them, but had failed miserably in fulfilling his promises.

He wondered how people like Mr Mohapatra, who worked in the same position as he, were able to purchase one plot after another in the city, how his colleagues were posted at locations convenient to them, and how they formed acquaintances with people in power!

The more he indulged in such thoughts, the more he was becoming aware of his incompetence. Even Draupadi would embarrass him with such questions at times. He would flare up and yell in exasperation. 'What do you want to say? Should I smuggle wood? Should I produce fake vouchers without even planting a single sapling? Should I illegally transport timber in government vehicles?'

After the initial irritation wore off, she would snuggle up to him and say, 'No…no, I am not saying that. Pintu is growing up. He needs you. How would we help him after he grows up? I can't give him any time. He is sad that he is not participating in any competition. If you worked here, you would take him to the competition venues. The dispiritedness in him would disappear.'

Debadatta would forget his anger. He would be reminded of his past. His father took him everywhere—to all fairs and festivities in the village. He would then say, 'Let me be transferred to a suitable location. You can resign your job, if you wish. Managing two establishments is proving very expensive.'

On meeting Debadatta that day, Laxman Reddy said, 'Sir, Conservator sahib is coming on a tour. The office has already received the message.' Debadatta had no knowledge of this. He said, 'Have you informed Mr Mohanty?' 'Yes, it is he who asked me to pass the message to you.'

Debadatta remained busy in preparing the necessary papers. The Conservator was a nuisance. If he got angry, he could send him somewhere farther. After all the Banei posting was not that bad.

ꝏ•ꝏ

Draupadi was finding it difficult to erase the memory of the dreadful nightmare.

That day, she and Pintu were returning from the market with Debadatta. Pintu was telling them jokes. He had learnt some of those at his school.

Pintu said, 'Yesterday…do you know what happened? Somu fed his tiffin to a stray dog. I saw him doing that. I said, "Oh! You are not eating the tiffin but giving it to your brother." But then Somu got angry with me. He said, "If the dog is my brother, the crow is your sister. Why else are you feeding them?"'

Draupadi broke with laughter. While trying to prove his smartness, Pintu had unwittingly shed light on his foolishness. 'Oh! You are feeding your tiffin to crows?' she asked with mock-anger.

Pintu said nothing in reply.

Debadatta sided with his son and said, 'He must have done it occasionally. The food must have grown cold, that's why.'

Pintu responded enthusiastically, 'Yes, yes…only once.'

With a frown on her face, she said, 'No no…there seems something wrong. Perhaps, he is not our Pintu. Our Pintu was never so heartless and irresponsible. I get up so early in the morning, only to prepare fresh tiffin for him…he feeds it to crows! My Pintu would never have done that.'

Pintu confronted an unexpected problem. In his childhood, whenever he indulged in some mischief, his parents would say, 'This is not our Pintu. There must have been some goof-up at the hospital when we got him.' Pintu would try his best to prove that there had indeed been no mistake.

While they were still riding the scooter, Debadatta said, 'Jawaharlal Nehru once faced such a dilemma like Pintu's.'

Draupadi wondered what the two had in common. She asked, 'Go ahead, tell us?'

Debadatta replied, 'When Nehru was the Prime Minister of the country, he went to a mental asylum on a visit. It was decided that one of the inmates, who had recovered considerably, would be allowed to go home in his presence. When Nehru got him out of the asylum and was patting on his back, the person said, "Who are you?" Such unexpected questioning in front of the reporters and cameramen rattled Nehru. Without publicly displaying his discomfiture, Nehru replied, "I am Jawaharlal Nehru, the Prime Minister of India." The person flashed a smile and said, "Okay okay…go in. You will recuperate after some time. Three years back, I used to call myself Jawaharlal Nehru."'

Draupadi and Pintu burst into loud peals of laughter. Even Debadatta could not keep himself from laughing.

Exactly at that moment, the tyres slipped. They were thrown off the scooter. An injured Draupadi somehow got up to see the three hoodlums, standing in front of them, armed with *lathi*s, chains and knives.

She ran towards Pintu, just as one runs towards one's money floating away with wind, and helped him get up on his feet. Suddenly, the young man with the knife in his hand rushed towards them and snatched away Pintu from her clutches.

Debadatta had received grievous injury on his waist. He was writhing in pain and crying out for help.

That bearded young man rushed towards her like a mad bull. He took out a *bhujali* knife, held it close to her throat, and yelled, 'If you act smart, I'll cut those two into four pieces. Keep it in your mind. You didn't see anything that day. N...o...t...h...i...n...g! What would you see when nothing happened? Understand!'

Draupadi felt as if her throat was parched. Not a word escaped from her mouth. The sharp *bhujali* still kissed her throat. She joined her palms in a prayer and said, 'I have neither disclosed anything to anyone till now, nor do I intend to do so in future. Please spare us.'

The young man broke the strap of her gold chain with the sharp edge of his *bhujali* and turned around to leave. Before leaving, he kicked Debadatta without even any provocation.

Draupadi got up with a start and looked around to see where she was. Was she at home or at the market place? She touched her neck wishing to wipe the drops of blood. Surprisingly, her gold chain was still there. Oh, it was a nightmare! How relieved she felt now!

She looked for Pintu. The child was still sleeping, unaware of what she had seen in a dream. Debadatta was safe at Phulbani.

She got up, went to the dining table, gulped down a few glasses of cold water, and returned to bed. Despite the best of her efforts, the nightmare showed no signs of receding from her mind. She prayed to Lord Jagannath, 'O Lord, guide me out of this trouble. Only you can protect us.'

Dawn was a few hours away. Draupadi did not switch off the lights. Sleep eluded her eyes. She reminded herself of all the stories she had heard about dacoits and murderers.

These people run a systematic racket. They are hand in gloves with the police. Why should they care for others, then?

Kalpana had told her once how the jail guards allowed selected thieves to go on their missions at night. The thieves kept half of the booty whereas the guards took the remaining portion. Such thieves are hardly caught. If they are apprehended, they take the blame upon themselves. They confess that they were running away from the prisons by jumping over the high walls.

Draupadi also thought of the mafia dons whom she had seen in the films. How calm, quiet and peaceful they appear! They speak and behave like gentlemen. However, everybody dances to their tunes. Their orders are carried out forthwith. They can shoot someone in the wink of an eye. They leave the spot of the crime nonchalantly, with a smile playing on their lips, without any regrets.

Bhubaneswar was no more a safe place for residents. She had heard that even Dawood was eyeing this city to carry out his criminal activities. Draupadi had read in the newspapers that he had a hand in the murder of the cassette king Gulsan Kumar. 'How a person, living far away from this country, could kill human beings, blow away high-rise buildings, and derail trains?' she wondered at times. Was he so immensely powerful? Debadatta had told her once, 'He is the mastermind of a huge racket. Dawood lives in Dubai. However, those who work for him and carry out his missions can be found all over this country—in Mumbai, Delhi, Kolkata. These people are controlled remotely. They receive instructions through code-words. The network is managed by hardcore criminals with the help of petty criminals. Even he has employed spies, who pass him the necessary information on payment. Once the target is fixed, the operation starts. Depending on the amount of *supari*, arrangements are made.'

'*Supari*! What do you mean by that?'

'Price! Like for a contract murder. The price fixed for killing someone. Dawood does not always kill people for his own selfish motives. At times, he works for others for money. He is no less than Lord Yamaraj. If you want to get someone eliminated, just give a photo and the *supari*. They eliminate the person for you. Money matters! Why should he kill someone without being paid adequately?'

Draupadi shivered in terror. The daughter of an honest teacher, she was brought up in a village. During her school days she had prayed to God, 'O Lord, lead me down the path of truth and dharma.' The thought of savage violence was enough to make her withdraw and coil like a millipede. 'Did such people, who butcher human beings like goats and sheep, really exist?' she would wonder.

She had recently read that Dawood had eyed the Srimandir. He would get it bombed and demolished.

How worried she had become on reading the news item! How can he even think of demolishing a temple that is so dear to the hearts of millions of people all over the world? If the temple is demolished, would Puri retain its sanctity? Would the sea beach attract people anymore? She prayed, 'Lord Jagannath, please protect yourself. These wretched people can go to any extent to fulfil their selfish ends.'

She understood that people like Dawood owned billions of dollars. They could do anything they wished. They were second Gods. They could kill human beings for sport.

The nightmare continued to haunt her. The fragrance of *madhumalti* flowers wafted inside. A black drongo beat its tiny wings and flew up, like a black kite. She got up, and stood before the mirror. Drops of sweat appeared on her forehead. While she wiped the drops with the hem of her sari, the vermillion on her forehead was also wiped off. She breathlessly rushed to the bathroom.

She found fault with the political leaders and blamed them for all kinds of mischief. They gather young men and seek their help at the time of elections. They pay them money, feed them mutton and chicken, and use them to do their bidding during the election. When fighting erupts, these young men work as a safety-net. Draupadi's cousin Gagan is one such young man. The poor fellow has neither a job nor any source of income. When the election time approaches, he puts on a white *panjabi* over his jeans and roams around the streets. He takes great pride in being called a follower of Madan Samantray. After the election results are declared, Samantray conveniently forgets all about Gagan. Gagan finds it difficult to forget the taste of sumptuous dishes and demands his mother to give him the same. The boiled rice and mixed vegetables fail to satisfy him. Almost every day, the mother and son fight over this.

Draupadi finds no fault with Gagan.

He was a young man, bubbling with enthusiasm. He had his own dreams and aspirations.

Had he got the inspiration from someone else, he could have become a good farmer, or even a good player. He saw an idol in Madan Samantray and became a political activist.

Almost every other day, Gagan fought with someone. Consequently, he spent more than six months every year in jail. His father would mortgage some property, arrange money, and get him out on bail. Aunt would implore him to mend ways. He hardly defied her. He would mend his behaviour for a month or two, before relapsing into his old wicked ways.

He danced to the tune of Madan Samantray. His words were sacrosanct for him. If Madan instructed that he should tie his parents up with a piece of rope and beat them black and blue, he would do so without the slightest hesitation. Madan's free supply of wine, opium and ganja sustained him.

Draupadi's heart felt heavy. Why should she unnecessarily bother about Gagan? Weren't her own problems sufficient to bug her down? She should rather concentrate on how to wriggle out of her own problems.

That day, when she emerged from the bathroom, Pintu was talking to someone. She only heard him shouting 'hello hello' into the mouth piece. She snatched the phone from him and blurted out 'hello'.

By then, the phone had been disconnected.

'Who was it? What did he want?'

Still sleepy, Pintu mumbled, 'Someone was looking for the police. Must be a wrong number.'

She dropped down on his bed. She warned him, 'I am warning you. Don't pick up the phone in my absence, ever.'

Pintu tumbled into the bed once again. He was still sleepy. She fondly tousled his hair and said, 'Get up, it's already seven.'

'Yes, getting up. Five minutes more please…'

Draupadi was busy making plans for the entire day. She had to meet Mr Senapati anyhow. Besides, she had to visit the ashram and speak to Guruji about her problems. How could she live in peace when the problem stuck to her throat like a fish bone?

She was not sure if Debadatta would be at his office. If she could contact him, she would ask him to leave for Bhubaneswar on the Friday evening itself. It would be better if he remained at home on a week's holiday. Pintu's final exams were going to start soon, and it wouldn't be possible to ask him not to go to school. Unless a maid was hired, she would not be able to carry outher responsibilities anymore.

Pintu said, 'Maa, what are you looking for?'

While scrounging through the dressing table drawer, she said, 'Nothing. Get up and mind your business. Why can't you take care of yourself when you have already grown up? How long will you make this mother of yours suffer?'

Pintu kept quiet. He had no idea as to why Maa was angry with him, that too so early in the morning. He mumbled, 'I have told you many times to buy a bicycle for me so that I can go to school with my friends. Papa also wants that. Do you allow me to go there myself?'

'Enough! How can I allow you to ride a bicycle when you stumble while walking? Tell me, if a cow comes in front of you, will you ride in front of it or behind it ?'

The question was too difficult for the child to answer. He sat with his head bowed down.

'That's why I don't allow you to ride a bicycle. When animals are crossing the road you have to wait and ride behind them, and not in front of them. This is because animals usually move forward. If you ride in front of them, there is the possibility of their dashing against you. Do you understand? Go and prepare yourself for school. We have to start early today.'

While leaving for the wash-basin, Pintu shouted, 'I have drills class today. I need to put on white shoes.'

'Okay.'

Someone was standing at the gate. The absent-minded Draupadi opened the door and went towards him. She found the newspaper boy waiting for her.

'What are you waiting for?'

'You had promised to pay the last month's bill today.'

'Not today. I am busy. Please come and meet me on Sunday.' She sent the newspaper boy away, muttering, 'What a disgusting fellow! How he peeps into the house under the pretext of collecting the monthly bill!' She looked around and saw a couple of young men standing in front of Mr Sasmal's house. 'Oh, look how these boys gather like crows and chatter the whole day! Don't they have anything worthwhile to do?' she mumbled to herself irritated, and rushed back inside.

Daylight spread everywhere. The residents of the colony were busy at work. Happy school-going children ran helter-skelter. All this failed to delight Draupadi. A sense of anger and disgust was gradually coagulating into sobs. How could people indulge in so much merrymaking when she was in such deep distress? Who would she open her heart to and tell what went on there?

Who cares for others in this world! Everybody is busy in his own affairs. She consoled herself and sat down to iron Pintu's uniform.

Pintu was mumbling a song in the bathroom. Draupadi shouted, 'Hurry up, dear. We are getting late.'

The singing stopped abruptly.

Everything irritated her now, even songs and smiles. She felt as if a pointed sword was perennially hanging over her head. What a great blunder she had committed that moment! Like all others, she could have taken a detour and gone away unconcerned. Her momentary decision to react was causing all the trouble.

Even Rahim, the rickshaw-puller, was nowhere to be seen. He had gone somewhere since Wednesday. Was he passing information to the hoodlums about her family? Mr Nayak was telling the truth. One could hardly rely on these people. They are all agents. They appear innocent outwardly but inside, they are as dangerous as venomous snakes.

'Let's see what happens. I haven't revealed anything to anyone so far, not even to my husband or my son. Why should they be vengeful with me when I have caused them no trouble at all?'

Draupadi was looking for means for her own safety. In exchange for her silence, she begged for their mercy. She took out the bunch of keys from her bag and shut the doors and windows. Pintu sat in the courtyard trying to put on his white shoes. 'How can you take care of yourself when you fail to put on a mere pair of shoes? Do you do it this way, with the strap on? Take it off first. Then put your feet in.'

Finally, she helped Pintu put on his shoes.

The Stewart School square was a few metres away when Draupadi's heart started beating heavily. Only committing a crime can cause such a shiver. Her heart didn't quake so fast even when, during her childhood, she returned home after a poor performance in exams. She sat firm. The noise all around didn't pierce through her ears; her eyes didn't record the sights and scenes. She held Pintu firmly with one hand. She feared that someone might try to snatch her from Pintu or snatch Pintu from her. She just wished to navigate the time and distance.

All those who crossed her from right or left appeared like murderers. As if they all looked at her and at her son with wide eyes. She was trying her best to get away from those frightening eyes.

What a time she had been going through for the last four days! While at office, she feared they might have broken into her house and damaged all the household articles. While at home, instead of avoiding a call, she was waiting breathlessly for the telephone bell to ring. She was even ready to fall at the feet of the caller, if he identified himself as the murderer and not a police officer. 'Trust me, I have divulged nothing to anybody,' was the explanation she gave to the imagined caller.

Suddenly Pintu said, 'Stop, stop. We have reached our school.'

This startled an absent-minded Draupadi. Heaving a deep sigh, she handed over Pintu his water-bottle. As usual she said, 'Be careful. Wait for me. Don't go anywhere. I'll come at 4 and take you back.'

Pintu said goodbye and entered the school gate.

Draupadi waved her hands only, she preferred not a word to escape through her lips.

That morning, she had been looking for the charmed talisman her mother had given her. She had kept it somewhere. Her mother had said, 'It is charmed by Siddhakapali. He performed *pooja* in the cremation ground for days and charmed it by virtue of his special powers. The user will not be humbled by ghosts and spirits, and even thieves and dacoits.'

That day she had smiled at the words of her mother. Just to satisfy her, she had put it on, only to take it off upon reaching Bhubaneswar. Now she had misplaced it.

On reaching the ashram, Draupadi saw that it was almost deserted. She took off her shoes, left them near the gate, and rang the temple bell. She covered her head with the *aanchal* of her saree and knelt down before the deity in reverence. How pious was the atmosphere of the ashram, she thought to herself.

A disciple emerged from the inner chambers where the Guru lived.

'Is Gurudev in?' Draupadi asked.

'No, he has already left for Benaras. He will return next Friday,' said the disciple and left.

The world suddenly grew dark. The astrological predictions in the newspaper were proving true. The talisman could have provided some protection but it was missing. Gurudev had asked her to meet him in the evening but when she reached his abode in the morning, he was already gone. What could these be, if not portents of calamity? Crestfallen, she left the ashram.

The rickshaw-puller asked, 'Where are we going now, madam?'

'Telephone Bhawan.'

Even Mr Senapati had not reached the office. The gentleman always said that he reached office by nine. Although it was forty-five minutes past nine already, there was no sign of him. Draupadi waited anxiously.

Perhaps discussing the matter with Kalpana's husband would be of some help, she thought. He had been working in Bihar for quite some time. Such things must be very common there. He could be of some help.

'But…but…if the bastards get an inkling of it!'

The wait for Mr Senapati was getting longer and she was getting late. She thought of going to office first and then ringing up Mr Senapati from there. But there were two problems about that. It was difficult to contact Mr Senapati on phone as both his phones remained engaged most of the time. Secondly, he would not accord the same importance to her problem if they talked over phone.

Draupadi spent some time waiting in the corridor. Her eyes were focused on the gate, the cycle and scooter stand beyond it, and the boundary wall. Her eyes fell on an elderly gentleman peeing exactly at the same spot where prohibitory messages were written, both in English and Odia. She turned her gaze away in embarrassment. Hasn't someone rightly said, 'Prohibitions are provocations'?

The crowd at the Telephone Bhawan was thickening as time passed. The visitors were looking at Draupadi as if she was a strange animal in a zoo. 'Why do people ogle at lone women like this? They behave as if they have never seen a woman earlier and do not have the possibility of meeting one in future!' she felt vexed. The Audit Party had already reached at her office to carry out audit on accounts. Strange people... create unnecessary trouble for others.

Draupadi was dithering about what to do when she saw Mr Senapati approach from a distance. She thought, 'Thank God for saving my efforts and time!'

The moment Mr Senapati's eyes fell on her, he said, 'I tried but could not trace the number.'

'What do you mean?' Draupadi appeared a little perturbed.

'There could be two possibilities. Either the telephone official was absent at the exchange, or the hoodlum rang up from a public call office.'

'But you had promised...'

Mr Senapati appeared a little solemn. He said, 'Madam, I am trying. Officially, I can't help. I have only requested them. If you want, you can submit an application. We shall see what can be done then.'

Mr Senapati pushed the door of his room open and entered inside.

Draupadi felt insulted and depressed. She returned to her rickshaw. The rickshaw-puller was some distance away, smoking a *bidi* at a roadside shop.

The moment she stepped into the office, Mr Nayak said, 'Madam, the BM has been looking for you. Please meet him immediately.'

Draupadi looked at the wall-clock. It was about 11. Placing her handbag in a drawer, she hurried to meet the BM.

Debadatta had no idea how the responsibility of arranging the dinner on the occasion of the conservator's visit rested in the hands of Digal, and not their office.

He had laughed silently when he heard that the Conservator was scheduled to visit them on an official tour, accompanied by his wife. If the Prime Ministers and Chief Ministers can visit countries like America and England with their spouse and children, why can't the Conservator tour Phulbani with his spouse?

Displaying his magnanimity, the Conservator proudly announced the reason for her arrival, 'She loves forests, you know? That's why...' Debadatta feigned being grateful to hear that. Digal said, 'Madam, the dense forests of yesteryears have all disappeared. There was a time when the wild animals roamed on the highway.'

'Really?' blurted out Madam. Her lipstick-smeared lips and sharp eyebrows were raised in great wonder.

Debadatta thought to himself, 'Digal, people like you are responsible for depleting the forest every day. Why blame anyone else?' However, no such remark found expression for him. Although Digal moved around him he hardly took notice of his presence. For him Debadatta didn't exist.

Debadatta knew Digal quite well.

People like Digal deliberately try to develop close ties with senior officers, ministers and MLAs coming on official tour so that they can use it to frighten the junior officials, and dictate their own terms.

He wondered how the high-level officials, despite being so highly educated, fell prey to such diabolical designs. Just because they receive the simple favours, hundreds of lower-level employees are compelled to dance to the tunes of goons like Digal.

Digal sat beside the Chief Conservator and discussed irrelevant things. After the former had finished dinner, he handed him over a glass of water and a tooth-pick. When he washed his hands, he stood by the wash-basin with a towel in his hand.

The Chief Conservator patted Digal on the back and said, 'How are things going?'

Debadatta felt as if someone smacked him on his face.

Digal replied, 'Everything is fine, sir, by your grace.' He then looked in the direction of Debadatta and said, 'If we are graced by your visits, we can convey our problems to you. At times, we fail to get a right person to get our grievances addressed.'

'Why?' asked the Chief Conservator. Then, looking in the direction of Debadatta, he said, 'Mishra, is there any problem?'

Before Debadatta could respond, Digal spoke in the manner of giving a speech: 'Like branches and leaves to the trees, we have always remained associated with the jungles and mountains around us. This jungle is like our mother; this mountain is like our father. We won't spare anyone who tries to loot them.'

Debadatta stood dumbfounded. He knew that Digal was very intelligent but he had never imagined that he could be so cunning. How cleverly he shifted the blame on his department and also, to him!

He failed to convey to the Chief Conservator what went on in his mind. Most of the time, Digal was found by his side. When Digal was not there, his wife would be there.

The Chief Conservator said, 'I am leaving early tomorrow morning. Do you want to say anything? Are you not going to Banei? Oh, it is a wonderful place. The Khandadhar Waterfalls are there. You will enjoy it.'

Debadatta was feeling pain in his head, but how would he express his feelings? He only responded with, 'Yes sir…No sir.'

The tour of the Chief Conservator was over. He arrived with his wife, had his dinner at the Forest Bungalow with Digal, and left early the next morning by a government car.

'Banei is a wonderful place! My foot!' The words of the boss rang in his ears again and again. Anger and regret coagulated in him, waiting for a vent to express themselves. He sat leaning against a wall.

Those who come on a visit to such areas sermonise like this. 'How enchanting the mountains, the fountains, the saal forests, and the mahua forests are! During the rainy season or the winter months—one lives a full and fulfilled life here. How can you even think of despising it?' Never-ending sermons!

Debadatta knew that occasional visitors, who came on a picnic for a day or two, found the beauty of the place enchanting and enthralling. Only those who stay a week or a month get a taste of what it means to be at Phulbani, Banei, or Koraput.

With the passage of time, the news of his transfer to Banei sank in. Although he was terribly upset at first, he was now reconciled to his fate. He wished to go far away from the area where Digal operated. His arrogance and vanity were too difficult to digest. Now that the Chief Conservator had provided him patronage, he would hardly care for anyone. He was like the true ruler of the district; he was like its minister. He could both create a problem and resolve it. He could organise a protest march of the Kondhs; he could also organise a peace march. Such people enjoyed unlimited power.

Debadatta met Mr Mohapatra near a hotel. He thought Mr Mohapatra might have taken his words to heart but it was not so. It was he who called out to Debadatta, 'Hey, how are you, Mr Mishra?'

Debadatta was compelled to wait for him.

Mr Mohapatra spoke as if he was making an interesting revelation. He said, 'How kind and generous the Chief Conservator is!' Debadatta looked at him, confounded. He failed to understand how he had formed such opinion of him.

Mr Mohapatra said, 'Did you ask him about your leave?'

'Yes.'

'He must have sanctioned it immediately. A very nice person.'

Debadatta hissed through gritted teeth, 'No!'

'What do you mean "no"? Isn't he a nice person?'

'I don't know that. My leave was not sanctioned. He said that during the last five years he had not gone on leave even once. Why did others ask for so much leave?'

'What a noble human being! How precious his words sound!'

'You know, Stalin had once spoken like this. He never took even a day's leave. He didn't want people to know that Russia would not suffer hell in his absence. The Chief Conservator is a man of that sort.'

Mr Mohapatra found Debadatta's arguments too difficult to accept. He repeated his previous statement about the Chief Conservator and left.

Debadatta thought if he could visit different places on official tour with Draupadi, he would never need any leave; if he had a couple of attendants working at his residence round the clock, he would not need any leave; and if his orders were carried out the moment they were given, he would not need any leave.

He concentrated his thoughts on Mr Mohapatra for a moment. 'What had the Chief Conservator done for him to deserve so much praise!' he wondered.

What a fortunate lady the Chief Conservator's wife is! She could go anywhere she wished with her husband.

Over the last several years, Debadatta had not been able to take his wife and son on a vacation. Whenever he visited them, he would have a hearty meal and fall asleep. Strangely, his eyes would always be heavy with sleep; his body would be aching with fatigue. He would hardly wish to leave bed and go anywhere. In the meantime, the cruel time would pass, bringing Monday a little too soon. He had to return to his place of work. Even though he visited the market, he hardly took his wife and child with him.

Now, he had been transferred to Banei. When the Chief Conservator spoke about Khandadhar, he wanted to speak about the speciality of Banei—the mosquitoes. Earlier, there were no good roads. One had to take a boat to reach there. He had heard people say that, if the government wished to punish someone, it would transfer him to Banei.

For some obscure reason, he didn't want to go there. He also didn't know how his transfer could be cancelled. Who would do the work for him and why?

Debadatta was worrying about his transfer for some time now. How strange life is! When you don't have a job, you worry about it. After you get a job, you are worried about the place of posting. After posting at a place comes the transfer. If one is transferred to a not-so-suitable place, one bothers about its cancellation. The forest department in which he works has two ministers. If the minister of state makes certain recommendations, the cabinet minister objects to it. If the cabinet minister sends some proposal, the chief minister's office raises objections. Despite that, there are people who have contacts everywhere. How easily they get their work done.

All of a sudden he was reminded of Digal. Perhaps, he could stop the transfer. This Banei could easily be changed to Baripada or Angul. For that, he had to strike a bargain with him. Why should Digal listen to his request when he had done nothing for him?

Debadatta looked far into the road that ran in front of his quarters. On both sides of it stood tall, dense trees. The forest had a great variety of woody trees as well as fruit and flower-bearing plants. There are many who openly loot the forest. Some of them have grown extremely rich. There are many others who exploit the mineral resources to grow wealthy. Such people control the local politics. They lead from the front, with many others following them. They damn those who fail to follow them. The list includes poor adivasis, the underprivileged harijans, and some foolish fatalists.

Debadatta always found himself in a state of stagnation, like a traveller standing in a queue to book a ticket. He was not able to have a breakthrough. No one cared where he stood. He failed miserably to identify where the exact problem lay. Had there been something wrong with the social system, others would also be wasting away like him. But there were many who overtook others and forced ahead. Perhaps there was nothing wrong with the system; the problem created was of his own making.

The moon resembled the face of a worried mother. The weeping cloud had floated far away. Debadatta kept looking at the sky.

What would Pintu be doing at home? Watching TV or doing homework? Draupadi must be busy in doing household chores. Would she be thinking of him? How many days had they stayed together during the last fifteen years? One hundred…or one hundred fifty…may be three hundred days. Had he worked as a lecturer in a private college, they would have got more time to live with each other. Both students and teachers enjoyed too many holidays. He could then have gone home and taken care of his family.

The moment the idea of approaching Digal for his transfer came to his mind, he began to laugh. How could he even conceive such a bizarre idea? Digal would be lying, drunk and unconscious, in front of his saw-mill. He had dined with the Chief Conservator; his fingermark was left on his back just as Lord Ramachandra's fingermark was left on the squirrel's back; why should he care for an insignificant person like Debadatta?

No, he would never bow his head before that brute. How the other day he was threatening to murder his children and break his leg! Let others do what they want; he would never seek the help of such a rascal.

Debadatta suddenly remembered something. He should have rung up Draupadi and informed her about Digal's threat. He should have given her some indirect hints. Rogues like Digal could go to any extent to fulfil their selfish interests. Wasn't Draupadi a little nervous all the time? She would unnecessarily make a mountain of a molehill and put herself under immense pressure. Debadatta decided to talk to her about it in person when he would meet her next.

He was reminded of Mr Mohapatra. How deeply distressed he appeared a few days back! Was his problem solved? How come he was so happy today! A very cunning and practical person, he must have struck a bargain with his neighbour. Anyway, his problem must have been sorted out. Otherwise, he would never have been jumping like a squirrel.

Debadatta was making up his mind to leave Phulbani. He had to adjust his mindset for the Banei posting.

How diversified the experiences of people like him are who are frequently transferred! Thank god, he had not brought his family with him. There were many others who shifted from one place to another with their families. Just when you are likely to settle down, you get another transfer order. The vines you had planted just started flowering; the trees planted a few years ago just started bearing fruit, but you have to shift to a new location, severing all your ties with the place. This breaking of accumulative relationships hurt.

If Draupadi were a housewife, she and Pintu would be shifting from one jungle to another as and when the transfer order would come. Didn't many others like Lalit Mishra do the same thing? They would carry the burden of the entire household on their back, like a tortoise, and shift.

The headlight of a two-wheeler was focused straight on his gate. Who could it be? There had been no electricity at home since evening. He watched carefully. Some people were standing at a distance from his quarters. Debadatta grew suspicious. Could they be Digal's henchmen? Where was Laxman Reddy? Bloody drunkard! He must have drunk country liquor and lying unconscious somewhere. The thought of shouting for him crossed his mind but he didn't. He had a gun…and bullets too. What harm could these people do to him?

Those people stood there in the dark for some time and then disappeared. They must have been quite drunk. The smell of country liquor floated in the surrounding air.

How drunk these people could be! Outsiders consider these people simple and innocent but his views were completely different. There might be a few of them…deep in the jungle. But, most of them are clever…even, cunning. They know the value of money quite well. For the sake of money, they are always ready to commit any crime. He sighed deeply. Who knows what were their intentions!

He was reminded of Lalit Mishra. Mishra worked in a block in Sundergarh. He was in charge of the development of Pahadi Bhuyans. A couple of years ago, Debadatta suddenly met Lalit at the secretariat. He was looking very weak. He held Debadatta by his hand.

Lalit Mishra had not been promoted for a long time. The department had demoted him. He wished to meet the higher officials of the welfare department in this connection.

Debadatta was shocked. Why did an enterprising employee like Lalit suffer such a fate?

Lalit said, 'My problem is quite serious. Who would I tell it? Everybody believes that the adivasis are innocent. They hardly know deceitful ways. However, in my case things are taking a different turn. After a lot of personal effort, I had brought them down to the valley…from the mountain tops. I had convinced them to take up agriculture. I ensured that they would reap the benefit of all government schemes. However…'

'Did they all return to the forests again?'

'Yes, that's what their leaders told them to do. They said, "Every time you return to the mountains, the officers will run after you. The moment you settle on the plains, the government benefits would stop. The officers would get promotion and medals instead."'

Debadatta was astounded at what he heard.

'The leaders blackmail us. They demand money on every pretext. They are inciting their people and making our lives difficult. What should I do under these circumstances?'

Debadatta said, 'I know you are telling the truth but no one will listen to you.'

Debadatta had not met Lalit after that. The poor fellow! No one knows whether he had been transferred or was still living there a life of misery.

6

Mr Nayak remarked, 'There had never been such a weak government in power, nor will there ever be one in the future.'

The words, emerging in the manner of a speech, had impressed the Bengali audit officer. With the ball-point pen touching the centre of the forehead it was as if he was pondering over the solution to some problem.

Mr Nayak spoke again, 'The government announced implementation of the recommendations of the Fifth Finance Commission. This was announced on TV and radio. Newspapers printed it on the front page. Now, they have decided to withdraw it. Are these signs of a stable government?'

Mr Bose was nodding his head; like all Bengali *bhadroloks*, he was also interested in politics.

Mr Nayak continued excitedly, 'Whether it is Assam, Kashmir or Uttar Pradesh, the condition is almost the same everywhere. Forget about Bihar and what is happening there. What a farce!'

Mr Bose could no longer keep smiling. It shot through his lips like the betel juice through the *paan*-stained mouth of an addict.

Draupadi was not amused. If the work was completed early, she could live in peace. She was vexed that Mr Akhil had escaped on the slightest opportunity. Mr Nayak's childishness deepened her anger.

'However, your Odisha remains quite peaceful. After all, it is the land of Lord Jagannath.' Mr Bose said in a manner of congratulating Mr Nayak. 'It is but natural for a state in which a conscious citizen like Mr Nayak resided to be calm, peaceful and incident free,' he wished to say.

Mr Nayak appeared crestfallen. 'This is what outsiders think about us. The real situation is somewhat different. Just last Tuesday, a murder took place near the Stewart School in broad daylight. Those involved in the case have not been apprehended till now. Did the criminals come from Pakistan or Nepal? How come they were not caught? The incident took place in the presence of hundreds of onlookers. Still, everybody keeps mum. How selfish people have grown these days!'

Mr Bose looked at Mr Nayak from above the rims of his spectacles and wondered, 'Really?'

Mr Nayak nodded his head.

'How deplorable the law and order situation of the country has become!'

Mr Bose said, 'Even if the criminals are captured, there is little chance of their being convicted. In most such cases, there are no witnesses. Law demands accounts of eye-witnesses and evidence. Besides, there are hundreds of lawyers who make a mockery of the system. The country is certainly heading towards disaster'.

Draupadi was listening to Mr Bose absent-mindedly. She felt as if every word he uttered was concerning her. Just to change the topic she said, 'Would you like to have a cup of tea?'

Mr Bose smiled and looked in her direction. He only nodded his head. Draupadi failed to understand what he meant.

Mr Nayak said, 'Let me go and ask Prasanna to make some tea.'

Draupadi wished to take up the matter with Mr Bose. She wished to ask him if there were any provisions in law for the protection of witnesses. She thought, 'All facilities and privileges were for the elite. The security guards guard politicians; personal body-guards guard businessmen. What is there for the common man? Nothing. Hundreds of people die every day for no fault of their own. Their family members suffer untold miseries. The government washes its hands clear after announcing some compensation. Why should someone come forward and invite trouble?'

Mr Nayak returned after placing the order for tea. What a garrulous fellow he was! He talked excitedly today to exercise some influence over Mr Bose. He said, 'Had the country attained independence just as Subhash Bose had envisioned, and not the way Mr Gandhi had done, life would certainly have been different.'

'You are absolutely right,' remarked Mr Bose. 'Gandhiji advocated non-violence but fell a victim to violence, didn't he?'

Prasanna brought tea in three tumblers. She reluctantly picked up one cup.

The ledger and voucher files lay in a pile on the table. When were these going to be audited? Why did the audit party select such a time to visit their office?

Prasanna reappeared and said, 'Draupadi madam…a phone call for you.'

The word 'phone call' was sufficient to make her shiver. Her body moistened with sweat. Who could it be? She placed the teacup on the table and left in a hurry.

She wondered whose phone call it could be. She reached the sales section, picked up the receiver and said, 'Hello'.

It was Debadatta. He had been trying to contact her for the last four or five days, but in vain. He wanted to know if Pintu was all right.

The voice of Debadatta floating in from the other side made her intensely emotional. She held on to the receiver just as a drowning man clutches at a straw. She had many things to talk about, but surprisingly not a word came out from her mouth. For a small act of her foolishness, everybody's life was now at stake. She wished to apologise to him for her foolhardiness but could not. She only beseeched God to keep her family safe.

He asked, 'What happened? Why aren't you saying anything?'

Draupadi wanted to speak her heart out, but how could she when so many people were present around her? She was afraid that someone might overhear her secrets. She only asked, 'Are you coming tomorrow?'

'Let me see,' he said and disconnected the phone.

She was greatly relieved.

When she placed the receiver down, she found that the unknown person sitting in front of Gobind, was staring at her. A shiver of dread ran through her spine.

While returning from the phone to her section, she turned back once more to look at the person. He had still fixed his gaze on her. While scurrying back to her section, she bumped into Arundhati.

'I am sorry,' exclaimed Arundhati.

'No...no...I was a little absent-minded.'

Arundhati peered at her, 'What's the matter with you? You are seem lost in your head most of the time. You are not even coming to our section during the recess. Is there any trouble at home?'

Feigning a smile, she said, 'Can't you see…the audit party is here?'

Arundhati nodded in acknowledgement.

Draupadi returned to her section. Arundhati had noticed the change in her behaviour correctly. What could she do? Despite her best efforts, she found it difficult to maintain her cool.

Arundhati was a nice lady. Despite living in the shadow of a mountain of grief, she worked cheerily. Her contractor husband was a drunkard. He would snatch her salary to while it away on alcohol. That's why Arundhati had left for her father's place. The couple were not in talking terms with each other. Fortunately, they had a small child who acted as a link between them.

The world everywhere is full of troubles. Survival depends on how you cope with these. Had Draupadi faced one that others did, she would have happily embraced it. How dreadful was the trouble that stared into her face! Every moment she lived in great dread of the unforeseen. Someone might drag her out from her place and murder her. It was normal for hooligans to exterminate eye-witnesses. They had no compassion in their hearts. Otherwise, how would the butcher people as if they are animals?

Draupadi beseeched the deity once again to come to her rescue.

Mr Bose and Mr Nayak were still absorbed in a gossip. Draupadi returned to her seat. The tea had got cold. The two had shifted the topic of their discussion from politics to astrology. Mr Bose held Mr Nayak's palm and started reading the lines.

Draupadi thought of getting an astrologer to read her palm too. While she crossed the Market Building Road, she came across many astrologers sitting by the roadside. Some of them took the help of parrots to make predictions. The paper picked up by the parrot contained details about the fate of the person.

Draupadi hardly understood how this worked. How could a parrot, which had lost its own freedom, predict the future of another individual?

However, every astrologer didn't use parrots. Some of them consulted rare manuscripts to make predictions. Her neighbour had gone to Jhiinti Sasan and got his future foretold. The ashram had many ancient manuscripts including Achyutananda's *Malika*. The astrologer didn't utter a single word; he would only point at the lines written on the pages of the manuscript.

Draupadi cursed herself for not seeking this solution earlier. She had heard from someone that even a former Prime Minister visited Jhiinti Sasana to get his horoscope made. Even a former Chief Minister and many ministers of his cabinet also visited the same ashram many times. Why should people occupying such high positions visit the ashram if the predictions were going wrong?

Draupadi thought her mother was right. 'Your education prevents you from embracing your religious beliefs. That's why you are in trouble,' she said. Now she wished she should go to Jhiinti and consult the astrologer.

However, a devilish thought crossed her mind. What would she do if only vicious predictions were made about her future? Wouldn't it be difficult to pooh-pooh the predictions as untrue and baseless then? Mr Chitta once said, 'The sins of people with ill-luck can be expiated. They have to stay for a month or two at the ashram and do physical labour there. Digging soil or drawing water can bring them good luck.'

Draupadi fixed her gaze upon Mr Bose. A voice was speaking from inside her: 'This is a golden opportunity. Go and show him your palm. Let him predict your future.'

To her, Mr Bose appeared as the astrologer she had met by the roadside, forehead adorned with sandalwood paste, carrying the paraphernalia—an almanac, an old manuscript, and a magnifying glass. She got up from her chair, wiped her palm with her saree and reached the table where he sat.

Mr Bose said, 'Are you an Aquarius?'

Draupadi was taken by surprise. How did he know her zodiac sign just by looking at her? She inched closer to him and said, 'Mr Nayak, please let me show my palm to him.'

Mr Bose didn't read her palm. He only said, 'Madam, the Aquariuses are having bad times. This will continue for three months and three days more. Good days will come only after that. I am under a vow to read only one palm a day. If I break it, I will become a sinner.'

Draupadi returned to her seat. She was now certain that the times were not favourable. Otherwise, Mr Bose would not have refused to read her palm.

Draupadi was angry with Mr Nayak too. He could have requested Mr Bose on her behalf: '*Mr Bose. Please read her palm. She seems to be under great duress these days.*'

Instead, Mr Nayak's face appeared in her mind like that of a fellow competitor who had come to attend the same interview. Can he be called a friend? No...only a competitor. They wish each other the best but one sincerely wants the other to fail. Only when one loses, the other wins. This is the rule of the game. How can both competitors emerge victorious at the same time?

Mr Nayak appeared perked up like a winner. Draupadi, on the other hand, felt defeated. How can others be happy when she was under such stress?

But how would Mr Nayak appreciate what she was going through? She had not told him anything about her problems. If he had any idea about it, he would never have stretched his hand out before Mr Bose first.

She forgave Mr Nayak. Why should she blame others for what she is going through? What is destined will surely happen.

Three months and three days! Draupadi sighed deeply. Such a long period of time! Who says time flows very fast! Each day passed like an eon. She imagined how difficult it was going to be to pass the time.

Draupadi was about to ask some other question when the BM suddenly appeared. Mr Nayak and Draupadi stood up.

The BM said, 'I hope Mr Bose is having a good time here.'

'One who has worked in Bihar never feels inconvenienced elsewhere,' said Mr Bose. His words reassured the BM.

The BM flashed a smile and left. Draupadi looked at her wristwatch and concentrated on the work at hand.

All of a sudden, Mr Nayak was reminded of something. 'Madam, there is a letter for you.'

'Letter! It must be either from my parents or in-laws.'

Mr Nayak opened his drawer and fished out the letter. Draupadi opened it immediately. It was a leaflet seeking the divine grace of Maa Tarini, the embodiment of Shakti. It was mentioned that a poor man once printed a thousand copies of the leaflet and distributed them among others. He won a lottery. A rich man had to suffer hell as he disregarded it. The sender had made a request to make eleven hundred copies of the leaflet and distribute them among people.

Draupadi read the leaflet. As usual, she crumpled it and was going to throw it into the dustbin when she suddenly stopped. Carefully avoiding the curious eyes of Mr Nayak and Mr Bose, she put it into her drawer.

She felt relieved from a strange sense of sinfulness.

She had received such letters on two occasions earlier. The first letter spoke of some goddess in Andhra Pradesh while the second one was about Lord Shiva. Debadatta had burst into a loud guffaw on reading those. 'Must be the handiwork of some printing press owner or some religious fanatic,' he had said. If gods and goddesses could do so much magic, there would be great prosperity everywhere. Thieves and dacoits would not be ruling the roost.

'Do you question the existence of gods?'

'Usually, I don't. But I do at times,' Debadatta had replied mockingly.

Draupadi had no clue to this baffling question. Back at her father's place, she had taken part in many religious rituals. After her sister-in-law's entry, their frequency increased.

Debadatta said, 'The question as to whether God exists or not, is an old one. Many before you have raised this question. Many after you will raise it.'

'But what is the reality?' the young bride had asked him that day.

'I don't know. Some books say He exists while some others say He doesn't.'

He had talked about the dialogue between Gargi and Sage Yajnavalkya. He had also cited the example of Gautam Buddha and his disciple, Anand. To the atheists, Gautam Buddha said that God existed whereas to the theists, he would say just the opposite.

Draupadi took out the letter from the drawer once again and read it once more. She found 'in a week' written in big, bold letters. 'All religious gurus are unkind people', she thought. She should leave for home first and then decide what to do with the letter.

This time, she didn't tear the letter or throw it away. She couldn't.

7

Draupadi yelled, 'Leave it, I say, leave it… it will bite you.'

Pintu held a dog by its ears and dragged it. The animal refused to move even an inch.

She ran towards him and said, 'Do you know what will happen if a dog bites a person? You will have to take seven doses of anti-rabies injection, that too around the navel. Stupid boy!'

'These days, only one dose is enough,' said Pintu, pooh-poohing her words of caution.

Enough is enough. She rushed towards Pintu and released the dog from his clutches. Relieved, the dog whimpered and ran away.

Pintu fixed his gaze on the dog.

He said, 'It was unnecessarily barking at me this morning. I was going to ask why it was doing so, unprovoked?'

'Oh, really! Why was it barking?' She had heard the dog's cries that morning.

'It was not barking—it was wailing,' said she.

'Why do they wail? Do they also perform poorly in exams?' said the innocent Pintu with a shrug.

'What else will it do if someone beats it?'

Pintu said nothing. After a moment's silence he looked quizzically at his mother and said, 'Does it also laugh, Maa?'

'May be! I am not sure. I have never seen a dog laughing like human beings. The structure of its face is different. The change of expression is hardly visible.'

While they stood there, the same dog ran in front of their gate. It was being chased by another.

Draupadi reminded herself of the long wailing of the dog that she had heard that morning. Such wailings are said to be inauspicious and premonitions of some disaster. Someone in the family or neighbourhood might pass away.

Just before her grandfather's death, a dog had wailed like this in front of their house. Three days prior to his death, it would come in the morning regularly and give out a horrendous wail.

Grandfather was afflicted with a disease called old age. He was ninety-five. He had been bed-ridden for long. His prolonged care had made Mother wearied. When angry, she would blurt out, 'Oh God! How long am I going to suffer like this?' Mother's words would leave Draupadi sympathetic towards Grandfather.

There was a time when no one dared to behave in an undignified manner when the patriarch would sit in front of the door. Every member was respectful towards him.

When Draupadi returned from school on the third day of the dog's arrival, the old man had already died.

Draupadi and her parents had bemoaned this loss. They cried for long, although she had forgotten how long. Her maternal uncle reached some time later and consoled her. 'It's but natural for old people to die. You grandfather had grown extremely old,' he said.

Someone shaved Grandfather's beard. He was draped in a new *dhoti*. His toothless face resembled the face of a child. He lay silent, motionless on the bier.

Draupadi insisted that she would go to the cremation ground and watch his dead body burning to ashes. Her mother didn't allow her. Her uncle said, 'The soul of the deceased enters the body of the one he loved the most in life. If she goes there, her grandfather's soul would enter her body'.

'What would happen in that case?' asked an inquisitive Draupadi. No one cared to provide her any answer. Her grandfather loved her dearly. She soon relapsed into another round of wailing. She had been only eight years old then.

She asked Pintu, 'Where did the dog look when it was barking?'

'Towards the sky.'

'No…no…in which direction?'

'I don't know. He only looked at me and barked louder. It ran away when I threw a stone at it. But for your intervention, I would have tied a piece of rope around his neck.'

A shiver ran through Draupadi's spine. Why did the dog look at her house when it barked?

Leaving Pintu there, she went inside. Ominous thoughts clouded her mind. She had enough premonitions of an impending disaster. Something scary was going to happen; only if she knew how and when! She said, 'Pintu, you have already played for long. Come back home and be prepared. Father is coming tomorrow. He will ask you questions.'

Pintu didn't wish to go back to studying so early. His friends were playing on Mr Sasmal's terrace. He knew his mother would never allow him to go there. He said, 'Maa, I want to play for some more time…on our terrace.'

'Okay…go but make sure you come home before sundown,' said she, reluctantly.

At times, Draupadi realised that she was worrying too much about Pintu. If they had another child, she might not have been so worried about him. In that case, the children would play among themselves. Since Pintu was her only child, she pampered him a lot. Now that he was ready to take care of himself, Draupadi was putting hindrances in his way.

For the last eleven years, Pintu had been the centre of her attention. Only for his sake, she had been living away from her husband. To ensure his bright future, she joined her present job. She wanted Pintu to grow up and become a doctor. She had always wished to be one but could not actualise her dream. Her father fervently wished that his elder son should become a doctor. However, he committed to an MA after his BSc and joined a bank. Thus, their wish to have a doctor in the family had remained unfulfilled. Now the onus lay on Pintu.

Draupadi's life centred on Pintu's vocation, his studies, his clothes, and his friends. The child's schedules were of prime importance; she fixed her own into the void that existed there. Pintu's wishes were paramount; her own needs were secondary.

How they all exerted pressure on her those days to have another child! As if they had nothing else of import to say to her. Her father-in-law, mother-in-law, father, mother, elder brother, sister-in-law—they'd all crooned around her ear. She didn't agree.

Had she borne a daughter, they would have clamoured for a son. How would their family name be carried forward otherwise! She gave birth to a son but they still demanded a daughter. When the topic was broached, she would only smile. Was it possible to fulfil everybody's demand?

When Debadatta asked what they would do if something bad befell their only child, Draupadi appeared a little perturbed.

Just as a mother-bird covers her chicks under her feathers and protects them from the birds of prey, she covered him with the *pallu* of her saree. God protect her only child!

Debadatta consoled Draupadi. 'One should always be prepared for the worst. Would not lack of preparation complicate the situation?'

Draupadi was herself a witness to how her sister-in-law was made the butt of their entire family's sarcasm simply because she did not bear a child. When there was a marriage in the village, she would keep to her room, just as one securely kept the brass utensils in a casket, without mingling in the revelry. Just to avoid knowing glances and cruel scrutiny, she would never venture out.

Despite affluence, a strange void reigned in the house. Its atmosphere resembled that of a school or office. One had to submit oneself to unwritten rules of discipline. Not even an iota of indiscipline was tolerated. Draupadi often thought of asking her brother to adopt a child. But how would she tell them! She would tell herself, 'Let a few more years pass. These days women become mothers even at the age of forty-five.'

Pintu was playing all alone on the terrace. It was difficult to play all alone. Draupadi knew that but what could she do? Most of the children of the colony were mischievous brutes. They indulged in constant bickering. Besides, those bloody murderers might be keeping a watch on their movement, waiting for an opportunity to harm them.

She bolted the door and went to the terrace. Pintu had drawn two lines and was jumping over them. She watched him silently for some time.

Both heard a motorcycle coming to a halt in front of their house.

'It seems someone is looking for us,' said Pintu.

Draupadi smoothed her saree corner and looked down. Someone was standing near their gate.

She said, 'Pintu, let's go back now. It is getting dark. You need to study.'

She came downstairs. She switched on the light but to no avail. 'Oh, how many times the bulb needs to be changed!' she grumbled, went to the door, and said, 'Who is it?'

A hefty man was standing near the motorcycle. At the sight of her, he spoke in a solemn voice, 'Are you Draupadi Mishra?'

While dithering about what to say, words emerged from within her, 'Yes.'

'May I come inside and have a chat?'

The room was steeped in darkness. She said, 'You can tell me what the matter is, here. There is no light inside.'

'We have rung you up a few times but you are not picking up the phone. We need to discuss something important.'

Draupadi had become impatient by then. She said, 'Well then tell me what you want to tell.'

Suddenly Pintu arrived there and said, 'Uncle, *Namaskar*'.

'Your son? Very smart.'

'Yes,' she said. She gave Pintu a hard push as she didn't want the man to mark him clearly.

The man started speaking in a gentle voice. 'Madam, we need your help in the Stewart School murder case. We have been informed that you were present at the spot.'

Draupadi's body became cold like ice. Her entire body shivered like a leaf in the storm. However, she gathered courage and spoke gently, 'Sorry, sir. You have received wrong information. I was not there.'

The man gave her a surprised look.

She tried being curt, 'Do you want to ask anything else?'

'Doesn't your son study at Stewart School?'

'Yes, but why?'

'No...no its nothing. We thought you knew something about the case. If you say you don't, we have nothing to say.'

Draupadi kept quiet. The man returned to his motorcycle, started the engine, and left.

Draupadi shut the door with a thud. She gave Pintu another hard push and said, 'What was the need of going outside? Do you think you are very smart?'

Pintu failed to understand why his mother was so angry. His parents had told him repeatedly to say *namaskar* to any guest who visited them. He had done exactly what he had been asked to do. Nothing more. What made mother angry, then?

Draupadi felt very light. The man must be a gang member. He would go back and tell his friends that there was no problem whatsoever on her account.

How strong the network of the murderers was! How daring they were. She had read about such incidents in the newspaper but had no direct experience.

Pintu suggested, 'Why don't you light a candle?'

'Yes…let me do that,' said Draupadi and went to the kitchen to search for a candle.

She was amazed to think how she could tell such a big lie so calmly and effortlessly.

Pintu, in the meantime, brought his books and sat down to study.

'Just go and see if there is a power-cut or if we have some problem.'

Pintu craned his neck out of the window, looked around and said, 'There is light only at Sasmal Uncle's house; the entire city is buried in darkness otherwise.'

'The phase from which Sasmal Uncle gets his electricity supply is different,' said Draupadi and appreciated the former's ability to manipulate things. The State Electricity Board had been dissolved and the responsibility of electricity supply had been transferred to different companies. However, this has not improved power supply to their locality. She didn't wish to ring up to the fuse call centre to hear their boring excuses.

'What are you reading, babu?'

'About Sahid Bhagat Singh. My teacher says if everybody becomes brave like him, the country will be transformed.'

Draupadi felt as if somebody shoved her from behind. Irritated, she said, 'Why don't you concentrate more on mathematics? Don't you remember how poorly you had performed in mathematics last time? You had only scored 55 marks.'

Pintu set aside his social-studies book and did as his mother had said.

8

Every time the transfer order arrived, Debadatta would think of bringing his wife and child to him so that they could see his old place of work and spend a few days with him. They would roam around the town and form an idea as to how he spent his time, which hotel he frequented to have his lunch and dinner, the *paan* shops he went to, and the people he had developed friendship with. After that, he would drop them at Bhubaneswar and leave for his new place of work.

Debadatta's plans never materialised. For some reason or the other, the plans had to be shelved every time.

Once it so happened that his reliever failed to report for three months. So Debadatta could not be relieved. He was at Sundergarh then. He had thought of spending a few days with his wife and child. He had also planned to pay a visit to Maheswar at Rourkella. The last time he was transferred from Bhawanipatna, his family spent a few days with him. After they returned to Bhubaneswar, Pintu was down with fever. So,

Draupadi was not ready to take any risk this time. During the Rajanagar posting, he never wanted to take them to his place. Travelling to that remote place was tough. Besides, he had got involved in a conflict with the local political bosses; so he wished to escape from the place as quickly as possible.

Of course, he was not the sole cause of all the trouble. At times, Draupadi found it difficult to wriggle out of her official engagements. At other times, Pintu's examinations compelled them to reconsider their decisions.

After being transferred from Phulbani, he had planned to take his children there. If they had spent some time at Daringibadi during winter, Pintu could have had an experience of Kashmir. But the Adivasi–Harijan conflict took such an ugly turn that he had to shelve the plan.

Debadatta realised that only having a desire was not enough to visit a place. The local conditions were also a determining factor. Kashmir was gradually becoming an inaccessible place for the Indians. In future, students will have an idea of Kashmir only from the film *Kashmir ki Kali.* The conditions of Punjab and Assam are no different. An atmosphere of terror prevails everywhere. Within the last fifty years, the country has broken down into fifty fragments. Should not children be allowed to live in peace wherever they are?

Four years ago, he had gone on a visit to Kolkata. The Babri Masjid incident coincided with the tour. Oh, how difficult those four days were! Even today, he has goosebumps when he is reminded of it. Fortunately, Mr Bala and his family was with him. Mr Bala works in the OTM and they were all living in their guest house. They had to shut down the doors and windows for four days and manage with rice, *dal* and bread.

Debadatta saw Mr Mohapatra was coming towards him with a letter in hand. Before he asked anything, Mr Mohapatra volunteered, 'This is a circular for the golden jubilee celebrations. Our department has been asked to take up social forestry programmes at fifty locations. Have you seen the circular?'

Without reading the letter Debadatta said, 'Bah! What golden jubilee? Worthless things!'

'You seem to have lost interest in everything,' said Mr Mohapatra.

'If all the wealthy people and their children vow not to make use of teak and *sal* products in their house, the country will have enough resources for years. Otherwise, such celebrations are meaningless.'

Mr Mohapatra was enthused by the department letter. Without giving a damn to Debadatta's words, he said, 'Every department has its own plans to celebrate the occasion. We must do something too.'

'Why not? Does anything depend on what I say? When the order has come from the head office, it must be carried out.'

Perhaps Mr Mohapatra wanted to bring up some other topic but Debadatta was in no mood to talk. So, he left.

'Why these meetings, assemblies, and deliberations?' Debadatta thought. 'Does one need a meeting to plant a tree? People in my parental village plant trees almost throughout the year. In thousands of villages people plant lakhs of trees every year. No meetings are held there. But in a government organisation, no one sows even a seed without pomp and ceremony. Why this nonsense!'

His father was a tree-lover. He believed that trees were like children. He would take care of them exceedingly well. He would spend hours looking after them. When the tree grew up, he made sure that it bore a name.

Mother would always say, 'Your father is a crazy fellow.' Debadatta never agreed with her.

Debadatta had convinced Draupadi to come to Phulbani once. When he spent his entire life working in forests, what an irony it would be if his town-born child did not even know what a real forest was. If someone asked him if he had ever seen forests, he would point at Nandankanan only because that was as far as he had gone.

Debadatta now realised that, like most previous occasions, his plan was also not going to work out this time too.

He decided to hurry up to complete all the formalities before leaving the place. 'No need of them coming here,' he muttered. Was he getting transferred to a place of his choice to have fun with them?

Fun!

If a transferred official got an opportunity to spend a few days with his family, would it not be great fun? His friend Maheswar always made fun of him. He often said, 'Perhaps you have another family at Phulbani. That's why you don't want to take your family with you.'

Different people interpret his actions differently. Some say he is a fearless fighter; he is not afraid of wild animals. Some others malign him by calling him a drunkard, wood-smuggler, and heartless brute who kills deer and sambar for food. There are still some others who blame him for being a dissolute human, as if he'd befriend any woman and spend nights with her. Debadatta knew he was not brave. No government employee can be brave. Such a person can work for no one—neither for the government nor for the zamindar.

Draupadi complained at times, 'How do you people stay away from the family for so long? People like you should be sages.'

Debadatta does not find much difference between a sage and a man with a family. Both of them inhabit the same world. The sages are cowards and runaways. It is not difficult to be a sage; it is difficult to be a family-man.

One of Digal's followers was perhaps coming towards him. He had smallpox marks all over his face, hidden under stubbles of beard. His bulging stomach hung like a cane-basket.

Debadatta decided not to get angery with him. What's the use when he was going to stay here for a few more days! Besides, wherever one went these days, he would meet a few Digals. They outnumbered honest officials.

'My master has sent me to you,' said the young man.

'What for?' Debadatta spoke calmly.

'Sir, it will be better if the matter is resolved amicably before you leave this place. My master wants to meet you at your residence. What message should I carry for him?'

'Nevermind. It's okay.'

The young man was taken by surprise. He wondered why Debadatta was not angry this time.

'*Namaskar*,' said the young man and went away, taking long strides.

Mr Mohapatra came to Debadatta and said, 'Sir, there's no use fighting with these people. It's good that you dealt with him gently.'

'What do you mean?'

'Digal is the minister's man. He funds his meetings and arranges people. How will you benefit by fighting with him?'

Everything was crystal clear now. Digal has won the favour of Mr Mohapatra. The latter has shown him the way to deal with the problem. Otherwise, he would never speak in his favour.

Debadatta kept quiet. He was lost in thought. How can he allow Digal to escape so easily? If the Chief Conservator wants, he can release him at a stroke of his pen. It would not be possible for him to strike a deal with a smuggler like Digal. He knew he was going to pay a heavy price for his stubbornness. What might they do to him? They might unleash physical violence. They might target his wife and child. He might be transferred to Malkangiri. All sorts of such devilish thoughts crowded his mind!

9

Draupadi called out, 'Pintu, come and have your dinner.'

Pintu replied, 'Coming, Maa.'

The driver and his wife had been engaged in a constant bickering since evening. A disgruntled Draupadi mumbled, 'How wildly the woman has been shouting at her husband!'

The neighbours had rented out their outhouse to a driver. He worked in the Irrigation Department. Every day, he and his wife kept fighting.

The woman had been using slang in her quarrels with her husband. 'How could a woman utter such expletives without inhibition?' Draupadi was not worried about herself. These words were sure to spoil a small child like Pintu.

She served Pintu dinner on the dining table.

'No one bothers about others here in this colony,' she thought. 'Why did his neighbour think of letting his house out to such people? Wasn't he finding their behaviour objectionable?'

The tape-recorder was playing loudly at the *paan* shop at one end of the colony. This is where a group of young men gather to have sessions of gossip. They ogle at women passing by and whisper to each other, even pass lewd comments at times.

The calling bell suddenly rang.

Draupadi mumbled to herself, 'Who could this be at this hour of night?' and went to open the door. She looked through the peep-hole and found Mr Sasmal's daughter, Nita, standing outside.

She opened the door.

'Aunty, today's newspaper? Brother needs it.'

Draupadi had not got the time to read it. She asked, 'Is there anything important?'

'Advertisement by OPSC. I'll bring it back tomorrow morning.'

Draupadi handed the newspaper to Nita. While returning, Nita asked, 'Aunty, did policemen come to your house today?'

'Police? When?' a shocked Draupadi stammered.

'Father wished to confirm. Last night, Kar Uncle's motorcycle was stolen. That's why.'

Nita closed the gate from outside and walked away. Draupadi was lost in thought as to how the theft of Mr Kar's motorcycle and police coming to her house were related. Was she being accused of the theft?

She shut the gate from inside.

'Oh, God! How these people poke their nose into the affairs of others. So what if the police came!'

Draupadi grew a little perturbed. Was the plain-clothes man really a policeman? Did this mean she was in serious trouble?

She stood near the closed front door and shook like a leaf in the storm. A commotion raged inside her head.

Pintu called out to her from the dining table, 'Maa, roti… another one.'

His voice did not seem to have reached her.

He called out once again, 'Maa…roti please.'

Draupadi, as if startled out of sleep, said, 'Wait a minute… why are you shouting so loudly?'

She felt weak and drained. If he was really a policeman, her vigil over the last five days had proved futile. The brutes would get the message soon. There is every possibility that they would attack her during that night.

She braced herself to meet any eventuality. She readied herself to start an argument with them. She had not divulged anything to the police. There was no reason why they should be suspicious about her. She had not even discussed anything with her husband, had she?

She sat down on the chair with a thud. The bickering of the driver and his wife, the song from the tape-recorder, and even

Pintu's calling out to her no more reached her ears. The faces of the three people which she had seen on that inauspicious day became vivid in her mind. The cruelty and violence reflected in their eyes, their ruthless attack, and the bearded face of the young man sitting on the motorcycle—all played before her eyes like scenes of a film.

She was busy pondering what would happen now!

Kalpana's husband had an interesting story to narrate about murders in Bihar. 'Once they decide to kill someone, they would do it, no matter what comes in their way. The criminals would reach his home one night. The soon-to-be-victim, unaware of the plans, would be sleeping peacefully. They would knock at the door or press the calling bell. When the person responded and opened the door, they would ask his name. The moment they realise that their target is standing in front of their eyes, they would take out the gun and shoot him on the spot.'

Draupadi was busy finishing her chores in the kitchen.

Enough was enough. She just wanted the night to pass and day to dawn. Let Debadatta arrive. She would then leave with him for Phulbani or leave for their native place. She would never return until Susila arrived. If her anxieties continued to cause so much misery, she would go mad in a week or two.

Pintu was about to switch on the TV. Draupadi shouted, 'What are you up to?'

Afraid, Pintu said, 'It's time for the film, *Jaani Dushman*.'

'Nonsense,' said Draupadi, and switched off the TV. 'Go to bed,' she ordered.

'In that case, tell me a story. I am not feeling sleepy.'

'Just close your eyes and try.'

Pintu went to bed fuming. Draupadi realised it was not the right way to treat the child. She knew one did not fall asleep simply by closing one's eyelids. But how she would tell him that she had lost her calm, and that she was not in the right state of mind to tell him a story. For the past five days, she had not been able to take care of him the way she used to. She was getting irritated with his childish behaviour. Once the child had his father with him, he would report his mother's irrational ways. Let him do whatever he wants!

Draupadi switched off the lights, went to bed, and lay beside Pintu.

A moment later, she went and switched on the light once again.

The moment the lights were switched off and the room was steeped in darkness, ominous thoughts started troubling her. She went and stood at the window. She took a magazine from the centre table and browsed through it. She could not concentrate on anything and stared at the words to make sense, occasionally flipping the pages.

A gusty wind had suddenly started blowing. She looked out towards the sky. Although no clouds were visible, a storm was just brewing. She went back and shut all the doors and windows.

The ticking of the wall-clock sounded to her like the banging of a hammer. Lying on the bed, she reminisced about happier days. How calm, quiet and peaceful everything was! She would go to office, play with Pintu, watch TV, cook the dishes of her choice, wait eagerly for a phone call from Debadatta, and make detailed plans for the weekend.

How ill-fated she was! Mr Bose had made correct predictions about *kumbha rasi* people having to face troubles for three months and three days more. With only one day over, she was left with three months and two days more to deal with.

10

Debadatta took out some cash from his purse, handed it over to Laxman Reddy, and said, 'Please ask Mr Sahu to book a comfortable seat for me. Besides, ask him when the bus will leave the stand.'

Laxman nodded yes.

Debadatta continued, 'I am leaving for office now. Bring the ticket there. Take care of the quarters till I return. Don't leave it open in your absence.'

Laxman nodded his head once again.

'What a strange person this Laxman is! Never says 'no'. Always ready to oblige with a "yes"', Debadatta thought to himself.

He got busy packing. 'Had I received the transfer order, I would have carried all my belongings with me. God knows when the reliever is going to arrive. Ah well, let it be as God wishes. Next time I shall carry all my things with me.'

The sky was overcast with patches of clouds. It might rain.

Debadatta came to the courtyard and looked at the sky. He spoke to himself, 'It would be better if I leave for Chidananda Vihar and meet Mr Sumanta. He might be leaving for his village today.'

With Saturday approaching, government officials living away from their families, grew restive to meet their families. Booking a ticket and finding a comfortable seat became a cumbersome task.

Mr Sumanta was a lecturer in chemistry in a college. A fun-loving and high-spirited fellow, he would make fun of all those who whined about their Phulbani posting. This was how he played down his inner displeasure.

'Sir if not you, somebody else has to come here,' Sumant would argue with him.

'If the government augments facilities here just as it has done in Bhubaneswar and Cuttack, no one would find any reason to complain. Why to talk of other facilities, do we even get enough water in summer?'

'Do you think there is no problem of water scarcity in Cuttack?' Debadatta would say knowing full well that he was placing the argument only for an argument's sake.

Mr Sumanta, 'Only NGOs and your department people appreciate the facilities here. The chemistry laboratory of our college has fungus growing all over. Neither the teachers nor the students have any interest in studies.'

Debadatta thought that if Sumanta was also leaving for Bhubaneswar, they could go together. There would be someone to talk to on the way. But there was the possibility that he might have already left on the day before.

A vehicle stopped in front of his house and its engine kept whirring.

Debadatta guessed it might be Digal.

He was right. It was none other than Digal.

With a white *kurta* on, he looked like an elephant. None of his followers accompanied him today. He drove the vehicle himself. Debadatta got ready to confront him.

The moment his eyes fell on Debadatta, he flashed a smile and said, 'Sir, *namaskar*. Perhaps you are leaving for Bhubaneswar today.'

Debadatta was reminded of how Digal had threatened him the other day. In the presence of the Chief Conservator, he had been eyeing him as if he was ready to murder him. And today how sweetly he was talking! What a cunning chameleon!

Digal entered inside and sat on the tin chair. The chair was not able to bear his crushing weight. It creaked.

He said, 'I have already solved the problem of Mr Mohapatra. The poor man was in great distress.'

Debadatta had guessed it right then. However, he was not interested in stories about Mr Mohapatra. He cut in and said, 'Yes, tell me. What brings you here?'

'I have told everything about you to the Chief Conservator. The department cannot run efficiently without strict and disciplined officers like you.'

Debadatta failed to gauge whether this was a comment or compliment. But he appreciated Digal's wisdom.

Debadatta said, 'We have to conduct ourselves as per rules and regulations. That's a part of our job.'

Digal fished out an envelope from his pocket. He said, 'Sir, forget about the Chief Conservator. Such people come on tours once or twice a year. We have to run our business here. Without your blessings, how can we operate?'

Debadatta was well acquainted with Digal's ways. He knew how to strike the iron when it was hot. Not for nothing, from a mere coolie he had become a millionaire.

The envelope in Digal's hand looked like a cobra to Debadatta. It contained poison.

Debadatta said, 'Keep it with you. I will ask for it whenever I need it.'

Suddenly, Digal's eyes sparkled. He got up and hugged Debadatta. He said, 'I am neck-deep in trouble, sir. Everybody, starting from the lower-level clerk to those at the top, have to be satisfied. There are not many like you.'

Debadatta was reminded of how he had threatened him the other day. He felt like kicking him in the crotch. However, he controlled his anger and remained calm.

Digal insisted once more, 'Sir, keep this. Won't you allow me to render this small service?'

Debadatta patience was running thin. He spoke calmly, 'If you want, you can get me trapped by the Vigilance department.'

Digal said, 'But, why should I?'

'If I want, I can also get you arrested by Vigilance.'

The smile disappeared from Digal's face. He turned solemn.

Debadatta flashed a smile. When medicine becomes poisonous, only poison can be used to treat it.

There was no change of expression on Digal's face.

Debadatta said, 'You can go now. I shall certainly do whatever is possible on my part to help you. I am leaving for Bhubaneswar today. Please meet me at the office on Tuesday.'

'Please think of the losses I incur everyday as the truck lies seized,' said Digal.

'Alright, please bear with it for a few days more. I will do something on my return.'

Digal didn't have anything more to say. In fact, Debadatta didn't give him that opportunity.

Debadatta realised for the first time how powerful words could be, and that one can insult another even by not using abusive language. Words spoken softly can also be hurtful. He could not help appreciating the soul who preached, 'If someone slaps you on the right cheek, show him the left.' What could be more spiteful for the enemy? Don't react, keep calm.

Digal was getting ready to leave. Debadatta said, 'Don't worry. I will meet the Chief Conservator on Monday.'

Digal reached his jeep. Then he suddenly turned back and asked, 'By the way, when are you going to leave for Bhubaneswar?'

'Why? Are you also coming?'

'Yes,' answered Digal.

Debadatta didn't intentionally tell him the time of departure. He asked, 'When are you leaving?'

Digal dithered a while and said, 'At about 2 pm. If you so wish…'

'I am leaving a little earlier. Otherwise, I would have surely gone with you.'

Digal remained speechless. He joined his palms in *namaskar* and said, 'Please don't forget about me.'

Debadatta knew Digal was returning discontented. But there was no way he could give vent to his displeasure. It is an art to flash a smile but express unhappiness.

He kept looking at Digal's receding figure for some time. After he had disappeared from view, his repressed emotions found a vent to express themselves. 'Bloody thief, dacoit, blackmailer…intends to bribe me…humph!'

He got ready for his office. If he did not caution the guards, the cunning Digal would think of some plan to get his truck released. An evil character—he was not to be trusted.

Debadatta walked to his office. All of a sudden, he felt as if he had developed an attachment with the place. Whether it is a human being or a place—one is bound to develop a sense of belongingness with the passage of time. When he reached here a few years ago, he detested everything about the place. The roads, the shopping complexes, the green coconuts that they got from Puri for sale, the cheap cake of soap and the untidy people—he abhorred all. But today he felt completely different.

He raised his head to look at the tall *sal* trees dotting the roadside. He wished them, 'Let the sky take care of you, let the rains take care of you. The Forest Department has become a puppet in the hands of people like Digal. For some selfish reasons this have forgotten their responsibilities.'

11

Draupadi was running hither and thither in the school field like a crazy woman.

The fear and anxiety with which she had been living for the last six days, had not turned out baseless then.

Pintu was nowhere to be found.

Draupadi searched for him throughout the school. She ran from the office room to his classroom, from the classroom to the field, to the washroom, canteen, library but the boy was nowhere to be found. The nursemaid followed her from place to place and helped in the search.

Draupadi had waited at the gate for a long time. The school children took their turns to emerge through the gate. Since the uniforms children wore looked similar, she got confused a few times. Where was Pintu?

The crowd of school children gradually thinned. Students emerged in a queue. They were all older students. Pintu was not among them.

A distressed Draupadi ran to his classroom but found it locked from outside. A nursemaid was locking the adjacent room.

'Is he locked in some washroom?'

Such a huge building. Three-storeyed. Is he locked up somewhere?

She ran to the reception counter and yelled, 'Where is my son?'

The lady at first could not understand what she was saying. She asked her to cool down and then asked, 'Which standard? What's his name?'

'Gautam…Gautam Mishra…sixth standard.'

The lady asked, 'Does he go by bus or has his own arrangement?'

'Own arrangement. I take him back from school every day. But today he is nowhere to be seen.'

'Then, it's your responsibility. Had he been a student of standard two or three, it would have been different. He is in standard six. He must have gone back with some guardian of his.'

The school soon appeared deserted and bare. The teachers were found leaving the premises one by one.

'Did you scold him in the morning? At times, students run away from school in fear or anger,' the nursemaid was found asking.

Draupadi thought a little. Yes, she was angry with him once or twice but there was nothing serious.

'Is there any dearth of kidnappers these days? You should have reached the school on time. He is not here, he must have left. Search for him at your relatives' places.'

The nursemaid shunned the responsibility of searching for the child any longer and left. Draupadi returned to the rickshaw and asked the rickshaw-puller to go fast. 'Let's go home, quick.'

Marking the desperation in her face, the rickshaw-puller asked, 'Where is the child?'

Draupadi could not give him answer. Pintu knew she had the keys to their home. Why should he have gone there?

He had not reached home. The gate was closed, and so was the door beyond it. Draupadi returned to the rickshaw and said, 'Let's go to Kalpana's house. IRC Village. Pintu might be there.'

While travelling in the rickshaw, Draupadi was surveying the surroundings for any sign of Pintu. There were many children—some riding pillion behind their fathers or mothers, some in rickshaws, some going by cars. Pintu was not among them.

Did they kidnap Pintu as she had feared?

Draupadi could not think any further. Only three days ago, the kidnappers had kidnapped a child from the Shastrinagar area. She had never thought that her own child would suffer the same fate.

She was only a couple of minutes late. When she reached the school gate, children were still coming out and there was still a crowd. Pintu always came out late. He walked slowly and took some time to get out of the gate. She had scolded him several times precisely for the same reason.

Kalpana rushed out the moment her eyes fell on Draupadi. She asked, 'What's the matter? Why do you look so forlorn?'

Draupadi burst into sobs. Not a word emerged from her mouth, except, 'Pintu'.

'What happened to him?'

'Someone has kidnapped him. I don't know what to do.'

Such a problem was beyond Kalpana's imagination. She made her sit on the sofa and said, 'Kidnapped! How? Where? He might have left for home without informing you.'

With each passing minute Draupadi's doubt was becoming stronger. She was certain that those brutes had kidnapped her child.

Despite being worried himself, Kalpana's husband tried to reassure her, 'Let me get the car out of the garage. We shall look for him both at the bus-stand and at the station. If someone has really kidnapped him, they will take him there first. Otherwise, if they want to blackmail you, they will surely ring you and demand a ransom. Let's go. Fast.'

There was no trace of Pintu anywhere—Kalpana Square, Master Canteen, Vani Vihar, or Baramunda. Draupadi was looking for her son in every child she saw on the way. She was certain the abductors must have forced him to change into ordinary clothes by now.

Finally Kalpana spoke, 'It's already six o' clock. It will be difficult for us to search for him in the darkness. We should report the matter to the police now.'

Draupadi reclined on the back seat like a corpse. The fight that she had put up with herself to maintain a brave face during the last six days had gone waste. The disaster she had been expecting had befallen. Pintu would never be found out.

Her child, the embodiment of her dreams, consolation, and courage, was lost forever. He had eaten something at nine in the morning. How pitilessly they would be torturing her hungry child!

They returned to Kalpana's residence after the futile search was over. Kalpana did not know how to deal with such a calamity. Her husband was busy writing an FIR to be lodged at the police station.

Draupadi knew reporting the matter to the police would yield no results. On the other hand, if the criminals would come to know that she had approached the police, they could inflict more violence on the child. Terrifying thoughts tormented her.

She shuddered, deep in thought. Let her child be alive. She won't take the help of the police and lose him forever.

Debadatta's bus was expected to reach Bhubaneswar in about an hour. Draupadi did not know how she would face him.

Kalpana said, 'Drink some water. You have been crying endlessly since the time you arrived here. Don't be so nervous.'

Draupadi did not answer. Kalpana shook her but there was no response. She uttered a sudden loud cry, 'Hey… listen…Draupadi has fallen unconscious. Fetch me some water…quick…'

But before her husband could fetch the water jug, she ran to the kitchen and fetched the jug herself. She sprinkled a few palmfuls on her face.

Kalpana's husband said, 'Let's carry her to her place. Debadatta is expected anytime now. If he finds her absent, the matter may get worse. We have to inform the police, newspaper agencies, and TV companies too.'

Draupadi slowly opened her eyes. She was sleeping on the back seat of Kalpana's car. When the car reached Pintu's school, she yelled 'Pintu, Pintu' a couple of times, before losing her consciousness once again.

Kalpana asked her husband to stop the car. She got down and sprinkled some more water on Draupadi's face.

Draupadi lay immobile like a log. Delirious, her mind drifted in and out of consciousness. Many dreadful thoughts invaded her mind. She was busy questioning the Lord as to why she was being punished like that. Was it because of her refusal to have anything to do with a brutal murder that she had witnessed, and deprive the victim of justice?

Such feelings of sin and guilt invaded her consciousness. A thousand of such thinking coiled around her psyche, raised their hoods, and hissed around like snakes. The problem she had been trying to bury in some unknown corner of her mind was following her menacingly like a king cobra with its raised hood. In great dread, she shut her eyes tight and prayed, 'Oh Lord, please forgive me.'

Kalpana informed, 'Don't worry. We have reached your home.'

Draupadi looked around with wide open eyes. Over the last six days, she had only thought of the safety of her child and husband. She had cowered under fear imagining the violence the perpetrators could unleash on her. She had stifled the anguished cries of the young man helplessly seeking help, while bathing in blood. To hell with him! Was that young man her child or her husband…

She uttered a cry of great distress once again, 'Oh Lord, please save me from this situation.'

Kalpana wiped Draupadi's tears away. While cleaning froth from her face she consoled her, 'Have patience. Everything will be set right soon.'

The face of the despairing young man flashed before her eyes once again. A pitiable, agonised young man begging for help so that he could survive. How he beseeched the onlookers to come to his rescue! How hopeful he was when he fell at her feet! Draupadi, on the other hand, was trying to steer clear of the whole episode. She was trying to turn her face away from the streams of blood, tears, and agony to protect herself and her family.

That day, it was the young man's turn. Today it was hers.

Draupadi shut her eyes tight. She had bargained with her soul. She has to pay a price by losing her son.

Kalpana took out the bunch of keys from Draupadi's bag and opened the gate after some time.

Kalpana's husband parked the car, came running, and opened the door.

Mr Sasmal, his wife and children; the driver's wife were looking inquisitively at them. They all were curious to know what had happened.

Kalpana switched on the light of the drawing room. Her eyes fell on the telephone receiver. She wondered, 'Why is the receiver lying on one side like this?'

Draupadi felt drained out. She blurted out, 'By mistake! Keep it in its place.'

No sooner did Kalpana place the receiver in its place than it started ringing.

All three of them—Draupadi, Kalpana and Kalpana's husband ran to the phone as if it was their only source of hope. Draupadi picked up the receiver and shouted, 'Pintu!'

Pintu's voice floated in through the receiver, 'Maa, where were you? Why was the phone engaged for more than an hour. I am at Somu's house. It's his birthday today. I had talked to you about it yesterday. Uncle will drop me home. Bye.'

Draupadi felt as if thousands of butterflies were fluttering about her; gusts of cool breeze blowing from somewhere; drops of rain comforting her body and mind, her eyelids drooping in the cool breeze. She was running about in a green valley. All her cares and worries had melted away.

Kalpana asked, 'Is it Pintu?'

Draupadi's throat was parched. Not a word escaped her lips. Within moments, the colour of the valley underwent a complete transformation. An old woman, carrying the dead body of her twenty-four year-old son, whose face closely resembled that of Pintu, roamed around from house to house, from colony to colony. Finally, she reached her house and stood outside. She was asking her repeatedly, 'Tell me! Who killed my child? Who stabbed him so mercilessly? So many people were present on the spot. How come no one saw the criminals?'

No other sight was visible to her. Gradually, the old lady's shape grew larger. It enveloped the trees, buildings, water tanks, Udaygiri and Khandagiri caves, the sky, the sun and the whole Universe. In both her hands, she was carrying the blood-soaked dead body of her son, who had been beaten mercilessly and stabbed brutally by three criminals last Monday.

The figure came and stood in front of her. From several places on the nose, mouth, stomach and back of the young man, streams of blood kept oozing out. A corner of the mother's saree brushed against the dust. Her dishevelled hair fluttered in the wind. Streams of tears ran down her cheeks. Finally, she stood in front of Draupadi and asked her, 'Dear one, do you know who killed my child? My only child? Just look, how the absence of your son for a few hours has turned you mad. Imagine what I would be going through for the last six days. Don't I deserve your kindness and sympathy?'

Draupadi got up from the bed with a start and shouted, 'Stop! Stop!'

It was 11 pm.

Debadatta commanded, 'Just go and eat something before you sleep. Otherwise, you will surely fall ill.'

Draupadi opened her eyes. She looked for someone all around and turned her gaze towards the door. She reached the threshold. Looking strange in unkempt hair. The hem of her saree was brushing against the ground. She was hardly concerned about this.

A flabbergasted Debadatta watched her silently. What strange changes had come upon her! What was the matter?

She went to her bag. While she was taking out her pocket telephone-diary, her fingers touched a talisman attached to a black thread.

She took the talisman out. It was the one that her mother had given her. In great disgust, she threw it on the ground.

Yes, she had got the number she was searching for. She rang up.

Debadatta asked curiously, 'Who are you ringing up at 11 in the night?'

In a calm but firm voice she replied, 'Police.'

Utterly confused he stared at her with surprise writ large on his face.

'Why the police? Did Digal threaten you?'

She was grinding her teeth and muttering, 'Brutes… bloody murderers.'

Someone picked up the phone from the other end.

'Draupadi Mishra speaking. Please inform the inspector that I shall meet him tomorrow morning. I wish to share many things with him.'

Without waiting for the reply of the listener, she banged the receiver down.

A still anxious Debadatta said, 'What is the matter?'

In a cool voice Draupadi replied, 'Don't you worry at all. You go to sleep. I shall tell you everything in great detail tomorrow morning.'

She pushed aside Debadatta's leg, got inside the mosquito-net, kissed Pintu once more on the forehead, and said, 'How will you know, my child, how difficult it is to be a mother!'

Debadatta looked at Draupadi with his eyes wide open. He was not acquainted with this incarnation of his wife.